ZARA THORNE

ESCAPE TO SUNRISE COTTAGE

Complete and Unabridged

LINFORD
Leicester

First published in Great Britain in 2017

First Linford Edition
published 2019

A catalogue record for this book is available
from the British Library.

ISBN 978–1–4448–3972–2

Published by
F. A. Thorpe (Publishing)
Anstey, Leicestershire

Set by Words & Graphics Ltd.
Anstey, Leicestershire
Printed and bound in Great Britain by
T. J. International Ltd., Padstow, Cornwall

This book is printed on acid-free paper

ESCAPE TO SUNRISE COTTAGE

When artist Violet Brooke runs away from her London life and apartment, she heads for Sunrise Cottage. Safe in her rural retreat, she can forget about ex-fiancé Jayden Fox. The last thing she needs is romance — until she meets handsome Max Finch . . . As much as Max wants Violet to stay, somebody else wants her gone. But who? And why? Should Violet return to London and her real life? Or is Sunrise Cottage — and Max — as real as it gets?

1

February
Brick Lane, London, E1

The landline phone trills. I pad barefoot across the wide expanse of pale wood floor and pick it up from the kitchen counter.

'Is that Violet Brooke?' It's a male voice, young, one I don't recognise.

'Yes?'

'Hi there. My name's Jake Southern, from *Art Today*. I was hoping to speak to Jayden Fox. I don't suppose he's there?'

You suppose right, mate.

'Not at the moment, no.'

'We'd like to interview him for a feature in our next issue. Would he be interested?'

'No idea. You'd have to ask him.'

I'm about to put the phone down

when this Jake person with column inches to fill tries another tack.

'Well, how about I ask you a couple of questions while I'm on? It wouldn't take long . . . '

'No, definitely not. Sorry.'

I cut off the call as he's beginning to speak again, and pray he doesn't ring back. They usually do.

Suddenly I need fresh air. I wriggle my feet into my ballerina slippers, then slide back the tall glass doors and step out onto the balcony of our apartment overlooking Brick Lane. The girder-grey sky is alive with a multitude of tiny snowflakes. Resting my hands on the freezing balcony rail, I close my eyes and raise my face to the sky, feeling the pin-pricks of ice stinging my skin.

'Miss Brooke?' a voice calls from below. 'Did you know your boyfriend was involved in art forgery?'

Too late, I look down; and there they are, the same stalwart little group of journos who were here yesterday and the day before. Or they could be different. It's hard to tell, muffled up as they are in thick coats and scarves, with beanie hats pulled well down. All eyes are trained on me. It's not really me they want, of course. It's Jayden, but as he's nowhere in sight, they figure I will do for now.

One of them angles a lens at me. I duck back and turn to go inside, but before I can close the glass doors I hear: 'When's the wedding, Violet?'

I almost laugh. Almost. As if I'd marry a man I couldn't trust. I thought I knew everything about Jayden Fox, the East End art scene's hottest property. I thought we shared every aspect of our lives. How wrong I was. Not only does he have secrets, he's not even here to protect me from the outside world which has become a threatening beast, waiting to pounce as soon as I set foot outside the door.

Jayden, on the other hand, is revelling in the publicity. He has no shame, which is something else I've discovered about him, to my cost. He escaped prosecution — just — but since the media got hold of the story, Jayden has somehow managed to turn it to his advantage. He's rubbing his hands together, seeing only how the value of his work has shot up overnight. As if that's all that matters.

I make a cup of camomile tea and curl up in the red leather chair suspended from the ceiling by an industrial-sized chain. My hands clasp the cup. Steam rises. The chair swings gently, and the light catches the antique diamond on my left hand. I have no idea where Jayden is now. It takes me no more than a few minutes to realise that I don't much care. It's a liberating sensation.

My mobile plays its tune and I wiggle it out of the pocket of my jeans. It's Jayden.

'Hi.' I can barely bring myself to speak to him.

'You okay, Vi?' He doesn't wait for an answer. 'I'm on my way to Dulwich to look over a new gallery space. It'd be great for my exhibition. I may be a while. There'll be wining and dining to do, you know how it is.'

Which, roughly translated, means he'll be spending the evening in some club or other and will be papped falling out of it in the small hours.

'See you some time tomorrow, then,' I say.

Missing the sarcasm, Jayden gives an automatic response. 'Love you.'

And he's gone.

*   *   *

The tan leather holdall — designer, far too heavy to be practical — eventually dislodges itself from the top shelf of the cupboard and lands at my feet like a body. I drag it through to the bedroom and feed its gold-zipped mouth from the drawers and wardrobe. In the bathroom, I stuff the nylon pouch of my purple rucksack with the essentials. My art kit takes longer to assemble, more care to pack, but the whole thing is done in less than an hour.

There's no chance of Jayden walking in on me. He's not the reason I'm hurrying. I need to do this before my mind twists and turns, opening the door to fear and doubt and landing me right back where I started.

As my blue Toyota climbs the ramp from the underground car-park beneath our building, I see that the media guys have left, driven away by lack of fodder and the freezing weather. Even so, I stop in the street only for as long as it takes to programme the satnav.

For a moment I allow my thoughts to linger on the empty apartment. I think about Jayden's studio on the upper floor where he worked so hard to make a name for himself. I visualise my own studio, separated from Jayden's by a shower room and about a tenth of the size of his, but special to me. I think about our grey bathrobes hanging snugly together on the bedroom door. And I think about the red lacquered Chinese cabinet we fell in love with and lugged back from the Sunday morning market, on top of which now lies my engagement ring.

And then I'm away.

2

April
Fold, Sussex

A shadow appears across the grass.

'Sorry to interrupt, but I thought I'd say hello, seeing as we're neighbours.'

I'd registered a vehicle stopping somewhere nearby, but I was so absorbed in my painting that I hadn't noticed anyone approach. Glancing towards the gate, I see the front end of a royal-blue van parked beyond the hedge.

I twist round on the camping stool and look up at the man standing beside me. *Neighbours?* There aren't any houses close to mine, and I'm sure I've never seen him before. He stoops forward slightly to be closer to my level, resting his hands on his knees. They're broad, capable hands, but with manicured nails and smooth skin which hasn't been coarsened by rough work. My theory that he's the local farmer come to tell me I'm trespassing falls flat. The crisp pale-grey shirt and discreet navy tie I can now see beneath his waxed jacket also tell me I'm way off-track.

'I'm Max,' he says. 'Max Finch. I live in Clayfoot Lane too, along past the woods. My house is called Robin Hill. I saw you outside Sunrise Cottage the other day, but I didn't have time to stop. I was going to call another time, but, well, here you are.'

He smiles, which is when I notice kind, chestnut-brown eyes, slightly curling mid-brown hair, defined cheek-bones and a squared-off chin.

'Love the painting, by the way.' He nods at the canvas on my easel.

'Thank you. It's not half-finished yet, though. I'm Violet. Violet Brooke.'

He widens his eyes in surprise at my old-fashioned name. At least, I imagine that's why. I doubt he finds the name familiar, even if he does read the tabloids. Anyway, it's old news now, if it ever was news in the first place. I don't have to give him more, but for some reason I want to.

'I was named after my paternal grandmother. Granny Violet lived at Sunrise Cottage until she died, early last year.'

Max looks vague. He probably didn't know her.

'It's a pretty name. It suits you.'

My face heats up at the unexpected compliment. I wonder why I haven't bumped into him before, since I've been in Fold for almost two months. Max answers the question for me, as if he can see it written on my face.

'I'm away a lot of the time, on business. I was in France last week, but it's good to be home. It'll be a while before I'm off again.'

'I expect I'll see you around, then,' I say, hoping he'll take the hint and leave me to my painting.

I want those eyes and that smile gone. The fewer complications there are in my life, the better.

Max stands up. 'Yes, see you around.'

He heads towards the gate, striding across the hillocks in the field in his polished brogues.

I listen to the van's engine start up and give a satisfied nod before I take up the brush and pick up some Hooker's Green oil paint from my palette. Landscapes are my favourite subject, whether it's oils, or watercolour, or drawings in pencil or charcoal. When I lived in London — how long ago it seems — I would drive out into Essex or Surrey to draw and paint whenever I had the chance. Now, I only have to take a short walk to find inspiration; or, as today, hop on the second-hand bicycle I bought from an ad in the newsagent's window.

Half an hour later, I decide to pack up. I seem to have lost concentration, and it's nearly lunchtime. I pedal along the lanes, my shoulders weighed down by the rucksack, with the canvas and folding easel strapped to the back of the bike. It's a bit precarious but my struggle to stay upright doesn't stop me from enjoying the gentle warmth of the spring sun on my face and the colours in the flourishing hedgerows.

Sunrise Cottage is set in a slight dip in the lane, beyond a copse. Its red-brick chimney comes into view before the house itself, signalling a welcome before I reach the gate. By the time I've unloaded the bike and turned the key in the lock on the blue-painted front door, I've had an idea.

Inside, I drop my art paraphernalia onto the scrubbed wooden kitchen table and head straight out again. Max Finch has been on my mind since our brief encounter. For reasons I don't want to analyse right now, I need to know more about him; so, moments later, feeling like some kind of stalker, I set off along Clayfoot Lane.

The lane eventually emerges onto the main road, but first it winds past a field of docile, tan-coloured cows, loops around woodland purple-misted with bluebells, then straightens out as the woods begin to thin. Robin Hill — Max's house — is just ahead. I've noticed it before as I've driven past, and admired it. Built in Arts and Crafts style, it has mullioned windows, pointed gable ends and a red-tiled roof. Surrounding the house is an immaculate expanse of lawn, sloping down towards flower borders at the front, and upwards to a tangle of shrubs and trees behind. Despite its substantial size, the house looks cosy and lived-in. It reminds me of the houses in the Enid Blyton books Mum saved from her childhood, in which Nanny ruled the roost in the nursery and tea was served at four by a maid in a frilly cap and apron.

Now I'm here, I'm nervous about going too close in case Max sees me from the window and wonders what on earth I'm doing, so I stop just before I reach the perimeter hedge where, hopefully, the trees will give me cover. There's no sign of life, but the blue van is parked on the gravel drive, in front of the garage.

Peering at the lettering on the side, I make out *Maxwell Finch Antiques* painted in gold. No other clue, no juicy nugget of information for me to take away and mull over, but it's better than nothing. The man I met earlier seems too young to be an antique dealer — I tend to think of those as older men. I'm guessing Max is late thirties, which makes him about six years older than me. Why I'm bothering to do the maths, I have no idea.

Ordering myself to get a grip, I peel away from the tree trunk where I've been standing and am about to head home when a grey estate car sweeps past me, turns into Max's drive and stops inches behind the van. Feeling like a crazy woman, which possibly I am, I stay right where I am and watch. Out of the car steps a tall, slim woman with a swinging bob of shiny black hair. She's dressed simply in skinny jeans and a pale pink T-shirt, and she's carrying a holdall like a sports bag. Even from this distance, I can tell she's beautiful from the way she moves. She turns briefly in my direction as she locks her car. I catch sight of an oval face with perfect bone structure. Yes, she's beautiful. Stunning, in fact.

She walks up to the front door and lets herself in, and I set off home, grinding into the tarmac the sorry remains of my curiosity about Max Finch with every step.

★   ★   ★

It's not until that evening when I'm cooking dinner and happen to glance at the calendar pinned on the kitchen wall that I realise today is something of a landmark. It's exactly two months since I escaped from London and Jayden. That was how it felt at the time. Escaping, running away — it's all one and the same. I drove down to Sussex almost on autopilot, not daring to stop and think what I was doing. But I knew in my heart that it was the right thing to do.

I'd left the snow behind, but the cold that struck me as I got out of the car had been far more penetrating, the night blacker than it ever was in the city. Nevertheless, the cottage I'd loved since childhood and was now mine seemed to welcome me, and I'd felt a sense of pure relief as I closed the door on the freezing darkness.

The following morning, I was woken by the sound of my mobile phone. *Jayden.* I knew I'd have to talk to him some time, but in the event, he did most of the talking.

'But I'm not coming home,' I'd told him.

This was after he'd stopped asking me what he'd done wrong, why I'd left my ring behind, why wasn't I happy, and so on — questions he should have known the answers to without asking.

'I'll make it up to you, Vi, all of it, whatever it takes. Just get your pretty backside in that car and come home. Soon as.'

The plaintiveness in his tone nearly

floored me, but I'd stayed strong. The forgery business — and Jayden's other misdemeanour I'd since banned from my mind because it was too painful to think about — had brought me to breaking point, but they weren't the only reasons I wasn't with him any more. We weren't right for each other, simple as that. It had taken me long enough to acknowledge that, and I wasn't about to change my mind, even though a part of me still loved him to bits. He needed somebody who would drop everything and rush to his side when he clicked his fingers, somebody who was openly adoring in front of his public, somebody who would happily wait in the wings while he was off doing his own thing. And that somebody wasn't me.

It wasn't that I hadn't been proud of his achievements, or that I hadn't supported him when he needed it. I'd done all that, and happily, because I loved him. But success had changed Jayden, in ways I really didn't like.

I'd ended the conversation as quickly as I could. I was too churned up inside to talk any more, and I needed to have a good cry. I'd been stalwartly dry-eyed since my flight, but the dam had been about to burst — which it did, as soon as I cut off the phone. He called me once more, and I tried to explain how I felt, but I don't think he was listening properly.

I've got a new phone now. Jayden doesn't know the number. The funny thing is, he never once asked where I was. He probably assumed I'd bolted to Mum and Dad's in Leeds, and I didn't put him straight.

Sunrise Cottage is my secret retreat, my place of safety. But I'll have to go back some time — to London, not to Jayden. My life is there, my work is there — I teach art in various community settings, all on temporary contracts but there's never a shortage of work. My friends are there, too, although it comes as something of a shock to realise I don't miss them very much.

I wake up every morning to the sound of birdsong. My bare feet tingle with the dew on the grass as I inhale the sweet, musky scents of the flowers breaking from their buds. Each day feels full of hope and discovery. I'll stay for the summer. I think I deserve that time.

3

The members of my Tuesday art class settle themselves around the pushed-together tables in the village hall, chatting away as bags are emptied of pencils, brushes, pads of paper and paints. They greet me as they do each other, like a friend, which is lovely because this is all so new and so much more relaxed than I'm used to.

I had wondered how hard it would be to integrate into village life, but my offer to take the art classes couldn't have been better received. The last teacher moved out of the area over a year ago, and I'm happy to fill in until they can find somebody permanent. Once word got around, it wasn't long before I was invited to help run the Saturday art club at Fold Academy. The kids — well, teenagers — are great fun and so keen to learn.

My little teaching jobs don't pay

much, but it's better than nothing, and I do enjoy them. I'd like to sell a few of my paintings while I'm here, but I'm realistic enough to know that there's no guarantee of that, so I may have to spread my wings and find other work before my savings run out completely. Meanwhile, I'm enjoying the challenge and the novelty of living simply and cheaply.

Of the six women and four men in my art group, all ages and types, some are experienced artists and others complete beginners, but what they have in common is lively enthusiasm. There's a lot of chat, of course, and that's great because I'm learning so much about the village and its residents, just by listening. They're all so eager to let me know what's going on.

Today we're drawing things you might find on the beach. I've accumulated quite a collection, including pieces of driftwood, unusually-shaped and -coloured pebbles, and a rusty old boat propeller which I came across, inexplicably, on a grass verge miles from the sea.

'Violet?' Lizzie, a receptionist at the medical centre, waves her pencil in my direction. 'How about life drawing? Will we be doing any of that?'

The schedule I've drawn up for the coming weeks includes landscape, portrait and still life, using various media, but not life. I had considered it, but wasn't sure it was what they wanted as nobody had mentioned it before.

'It's a thought,' I say.

'We did some in the old class,' Malcolm, who runs a landscape gardening business, says. 'I made a pig's ear of it, though.'

There are chuckles from around the table, accompanied by nods. It seems everyone's keen to have a go.

'Okay,' I say, slowly. 'Who modelled for you?'

'There was that young man with the long hair and the muscles,' Marigold says. She's a retired maths teacher. 'I think he was a student after a bit of pocket money. I've never seen him around the village since. They drew me once, when he didn't turn up. I didn't take my clothes off, though. There's a terrible draught in this hall.'

'Small mercies,' Malcolm says, his face straight.

Everyone laughs, including Marigold. 'We had that lovely-looking girl with the dark hair a couple of times. She posed in the buff, didn't she?' Lizzie looks round the group for assent.

'Ooh yes, I remember,' Malcolm says, grinning all over his face.

'You would.' Lizzie raises her eyes. 'She was very good at posing. She'd done it quite a bit before. I think she still lives locally. I can't remember her name but I could find out.'

'Could you?' I say, surprised.

'Never underestimate the village grape-vine.' Lizzie laughs. Her chestnut curls bounce.

'Well, if you could, that would be marvellous,' I say.

A proper model is what we need, but I don't hold out much hope, considering how long it's been since art classes were last held here.

Lizzie's as good as her word, and a few days later she rings me with the name and number of our potential model. I look at the name I've scribbled down: Olivia Morton. Of course, I have no idea what she's like or if she's reliable, but if the last teacher employed her it's probably not too much of a risk, so I decide to ring her this evening.

Meanwhile, the cottage needs my attention. I inherited it from my grandmother, the bequest having skipped a generation because my father insisted he didn't need anything from her. I left the place empty after Gran died, intending to refurbish it at some point and rent it out, but somehow I never found the time. I couldn't bear to sell it. Sunrise Cottage has been in Dad's family for generations. Originally a tied cottage belonging to Folding Farm, it was sold off after the war, along with several others. As sitting tenants, my grandparents were able to buy it for a song.

Built of traditional flint and brick with a terracotta tiled roof and oak-beamed ceilings, the cottage was originally a two-up and two-down with a privy at the end of the garden, now doing duty as a shed. The living room leads off from the left of the tiny hall, the kitchen with its inglenook fireplace to the right. A narrow central staircase divides at the top, leading directly into each of the two bedrooms. One of the bedrooms has a twisty little flight of stairs leading to an attic which will be useful for storage, once I've swept out the cobwebs.

Little has changed over the years apart from an extension for the bathroom added on at the back of the kitchen in the 1950s, and central heating which my father had installed in 1995. He would have had it done before, but Gran took some persuading, insisting she was perfectly happy with the open fire in the inglenook and various free-standing heaters which she moved perilously from room to room.

Eventually, after a particularly freezing winter, she caved in, much to everyone's relief.

As I gaze out of the window at the tangle of garden, my thoughts wing back to the day Jayden and I moved into the Brick Lane apartment. We were so excited, like children. I couldn't imagine how we could afford all that space, let alone furnish it. But his career was in the ascendant, Jayden assured me, and as I had as much faith in him as he did in himself, I tried not to worry. We had our own private flat-warming party, just the two of us, and drank champagne from Conran mugs because we had no glasses.

I met Jayden while I was working as a temporary assistant in a small gallery just off Russell Square, one of my many jobs around that time. We'd acquired the work of a brand new painter, and Jayden, along with a couple of friends, had come to check him out. It was pretty obvious that they'd been to the pub beforehand; their echoing footsteps and voices drew attention, and not in a good way.

But my attention was all on Jayden, all six foot four of him. His thick, near-black hair had been swept about on top by the wind. With his largish nose and deep-set slate-blue eyes beneath a heavy brow, his looks were striking rather than traditionally handsome. Faded, narrow jeans and a tightly fitting khaki T-shirt gave more than a hint of the pleasures beneath. I'm afraid to say I stared, and to my mortification, Jayden stared back. And then he smiled, and I was lost. Even the fact that he called me Blondie didn't go against him; normally I hated that.

Within weeks we were not only an item, we were planning our future together. He was loving, considerate and ambitious — all the traits my parents wanted me to find in a partner, which made all three of us happy. When one day he came home with the diamond ring and slipped it on my finger without a word, I thought my heart would burst.

It wasn't long before Jayden's confidence in his ability was fulfilled; his talent was recognised almost overnight, his paintings were in great demand, and he began to reap the rewards. Jayden had his break and I couldn't have been happier for him. I no longer worried that we couldn't afford the lifestyle we'd set up for ourselves.

But as the art world embraced Jayden, I felt him pull away from me, and it was such a powerful experience that it felt almost physical. It wasn't a case of me not keeping up with Jayden, more that he didn't want or need me to do so. He had different priorities, different values, and it was so sad.

A heavy sigh escapes me. My mind keeps doing this, tugging me back to places I don't want to go. It happens mostly when the dark wings of night fold against the windows of Sunrise Cottage and the owls hoot in the woods. Night-time seems to emphasise my newly solitary state. Solitary, but not lonely, which is not the same thing at all. Lonely is too self-indulgent a feeling, and I refuse to let it in.

Bringing myself back to the present, I continue with the task of sorting through the contents of the cottage. It's a job I've only recently had the heart to tackle. Before that, Gran's home and her possessions still seemed to belong to her. But gradually I've come round to the idea that she wouldn't expect the place to exist inside a time-warp. If she had imagined a time when I might live in the cottage, she would want me to make it mine, and know that no matter how many changes I make, something of her will always remain here. Believing that gives me a warm feeling inside.

The kitchen, with its inglenook, deep enamel sink and jumble of wooden cupboards, has been sorted. Much of Gran's equipment is still useful, like the old-fashioned cream-and-brown basins, the white enamel blue-rimmed jugs, and the everyday crockery, patterned with autumn leaves. I've bought a microwave oven and a new fridge-freezer, but the cooker and washing machine work fine and will do me for now, besides saving me money in replacing it all at once. At some stage I'll give the walls a coat of paint, change the mint-toothpaste green for white, or perhaps pale mauve, in honour of our name. Gran kept everything spotless so there's no hurry.

The floor-to-ceiling cream-painted cupboard which fills an alcove of the living room — the parlour, as it used to be called — is next on my list. Its shelves are laden with 'the best' china and glassware. Carefully I lift out a dainty tea-cup and cradle it in my hand. Weightless as a feather, it's crafted from fine white porcelain, hand-painted with clusters of violets. There are six matching cups, saucers and plates, a pot-bellied teapot and a milk jug. Grandad bought the set for Gran when their first child was born, a daughter they called Violet, too. Sadly she died when she was fourteen. They had only one other child, my

30

dad, whom they named George after his father.

Replacing the cup, I take out another, of a different design. This one is octagonal in shape, and painted in incredibly fine detail with a pastoral scene depicting peacocks on a lawn and, in the background, a stately mansion set among trees, with a patch of blue sky above. The rim of the cup is outlined in gold and there are touches of gold among the peacocks' colourful feathers. I stand it on the dark green chenille-clothed table and carry on removing more china from the cupboard, from the same matching set.

Finally I look at the impressive array on the table — eight octagonal cups, saucers and tea-plates, an elegantly-shaped teapot and a lidded sugar bowl. This is no ordinary tea-service. Family lore has it that it was given to my great-grandmother as a wedding present when she was in service up at 'the big house'. I believe my grandmother used it occasionally when it was handed down to her, but according to Dad, it hasn't been out of this cupboard for years.

Picking up a plate, I turn it over, and there is the gold anchor, one of the marks of the Chelsea factory, used in the late 1700s. In the days before Gran forgot about the treasure in the cupboard — as, sadly, she forgot about a lot of things — she referred to the set as 'the Chelsea'. I remember asking my father what she meant. I wasn't too impressed when, on one of our visits, he opened the cupboard and showed me. China was china, wasn't it? Well, it was when you were twelve years old. The fact that it was very old and very valuable made no impression on me at the time.

My finger strays to the tiny gold anchor. Putting down the plate, I pick up a few other items and check the underneath. More gold anchors, as I knew there would be. I leave the tea-service where it is for now. The sun flooding the room makes the colours glow and throws out miniature beams of light from the gold.

I'm just about to head for the kitchen to see about lunch when there's a movement in the lane and I glance out of the window in time to see the roof of Max Finch's blue van stream past the hedge. It seems like an omen.

★　★　★

That evening, I make two phone calls. The first is to Olivia Morton. She seems surprised but pleased to hear from me, and yes, she would love to model for us. She tells me she's experienced and that modelling has always been a useful, and enjoyable, sideline. She doesn't say from what occupation, but no doubt I shall find out at some point.

The second call is to my parents in Leeds. They run a successful garage business together, and lead a frenetic social life, so it's not always easy to catch them at home. But tonight my mother answers, and we chat about this and that. Thankfully, she doesn't mention Jayden, London, or what happened. She knows we're all talked out on that subject. When Dad comes on the phone, I ask him about the Chelsea set.

'Would you mind if I sold it? Unless you and Mum want it?'

I hear him check quickly with my mother before he replies. 'It's not your mother's kind of thing, and in any case it's yours to do as you like with. It's worth a bomb, you know. So you go right ahead and sell it, but be sure you get the right price.'

I don't ask Dad what he considers the right price to be. It's not the sort of thing he'd be likely to know. I just thank him.

'And, Violet,' he continues, 'don't you go feeling guilty about selling it. Gran wouldn't have wanted you to keep the cupboards filled with stuff you're never going to use.'

This is true. It's also true that I can go to my parents if I need extra cash. The offer's always there, although I'd rather not take it up, and they know that.

'She never liked it, you know, Chelsea or not,' he says now. 'Thought it was too fussy, and certainly too posh to drink tea out of.'

I laugh. I know all this, but I had to make sure that Dad was okay about it. Whatever I make from the tea-service will be useful, but I can't help wondering if my sudden urge to sell it has anything to do with a certain brown-eyed antique dealer I just happen to have met.

4

It's Monday morning and I've just returned from an early trip to the market in the nearby town when a yellow, sporty-looking car pulls up behind mine.

'Need a hand?' Max gets out of the driver's seat and reaches for the bulging paper carriers I'm holding.

'It's okay, I've got these,' I mutter. 'If you could . . . '

'Ah.' He extracts the door key from between my teeth, marches up to the front door and unlocks it for me.

I dump the bags inside, leaving the door ajar.

'Thanks for your help. I'm all right now.'

I smile, letting Max know he's free to leave. He stays right where he is.

Nipping round to the back of the car, I open the boot to reveal a profusion of flowers. As the lid of the boot rises, so do the flowers, bouncing and settling again in a multi-coloured heap. A pink rose on an improbably long stem escapes and falls to the ground. Max retrieves it, presenting it to me with a flourish that makes me look away.

'Are you opening a florist's shop?' he says, pretending not to spot that my floral haul is entirely fake.

I explain they're for my art class. And then, instead of keeping quiet, my mouth runs away with me and lets him know that these are replacements for the ones I left behind when I moved here because I couldn't fit everything in the car.

Max doesn't miss the cue, mistaken though it was.

'Where did you move from?' he asks conversationally, as he ducks into the boot to gather up an armful of silk and plastic blooms.

'London.'

I've told no-one in Fold about my former life, fielding questions as vaguely as I can without seeming unfriendly. It isn't that I'm secretive by nature, and I'm definitely not ashamed of my association with Jayden Fox — none of that was anything to do with me — but neither do I want to be defined by him.

'The big city, eh?' Max straightens up, then almost topples sideways as he attempts to close the boot lid with his elbow. It makes me want to laugh. 'Quite a change for you then, coming to our little village?'

'Quite a change, yes.' I walk ahead of him into the kitchen, cutting the conversation off.

'Don't let me keep you,' I say, when the carrier bags and flowers are safely deposited on the table. 'Thanks for helping, though.'

For a moment, Max looks as if he's about to walk right out of that door, and for some stupid reason I don't want him to. And then he seems to change his mind, and leans against the sink with his arms folded, looking perfectly at home. Confidence in a man is very sexy . . . I stop that train of thought before it takes hold.

He shrugs. 'I'm in no hurry. I'm only going to the supermarket, the big one on the main road. Is there anything you need?'

There's a very slight raising of eyebrows as he says this, and it riles me as my mind forms a picture of the beautiful dark-haired woman letting herself into his house.

'Anything I need?' I ask stupidly. He's wrong-footed me now and my brain seems to have stopped working.

'From the supermarket. Anything I can get you while I'm there?'

His smile is genuine, his eyes showing kindness. I forget to be cross and my brain, thank goodness, forms a sensible reply.

'No thanks. I went yesterday and stocked up. Kind of you to ask, though.'

And then, before I think better of it, I ask if he'd like a coffee. One neighbourly gesture in return for another seems fair enough. Max obviously agrees.

'That would be great,' he says, nodding with more enthusiasm than a paltry offer of coffee deserves.

We have our drinks sitting in the old tapestry chairs, a small oak table between us holding the biscuit barrel. The table rocks on the uneven flagstone floor as our hands reach simultaneously for the barrel, making us both smile. I point at the cold, ash-strewn grate in the inglenook.

'Sometimes I light the fire in the evenings for the cosiness, but I don't bother in the day. It seems a lot of trouble, and there's central heating if I need it.'

'I know what you mean. I've got an open fire in the living room but I hardly ever use it. I prefer to throw a switch.'

Max's use of the personal pronoun gets my back up again. Is his gorgeous wife, partner, whatever she is, to be denied her existence? I'm not going to ask about her, though. His status, marital or otherwise, is none of my business. If he wants to tell me, that's up to him. But, neighbour or not, it must be time he was going. I'm about to stand up and clear away our empty mugs when I remember I have a perfectly legitimate reason for Max Finch being on the premises.

I take him through to the living room where the Chelsea is still laid out on the chenille cloth as if I'm expecting important guests for tea.

'There,' I say, pointing at the set. 'I'd value your opinion, perhaps not now but another time, when you're not in a hurry.'

'No hurry, as I said.'

He smiles, and I swear my heart stops beating. Max picks up the teapot, turning it expertly in his hands, looking at it this way, and that.

'The gold anchor. The Chelsea mark. It's there, underneath.'

'Yes, you said it was Chelsea,' he says.

He upends the teapot, holding the lid carefully in place in the palm of his hand, and frowns at the mark.

Setting down the teapot, he begins picking up some of the other pieces, a plate, a cup and finally a saucer, scrutinising each closely, top and bottom; and, I notice, feeling his way around the porcelain as if he's reading it with his fingers, like Braille.

He puts down the saucer he's been holding and looks at me. 'You're after selling? Are you sure?'

'Yes, I am. It's no use to me and the money will be handy. Not that I'm . . . ' I was going to say 'hard-up', but it doesn't sound right in my mind, and I've already given away too much. ' . . . I'm not sentimental about the tea-service, even though it was Gran's. She wouldn't have wanted that.'

Max nods slowly. He seems to be embroiled in thought. He doesn't want to get involved, I can tell, but he's too polite to say so.

'It's fine. It's not your sort of thing.' When we chatted earlier, I got the impression he dealt mainly in furniture, silver, and unusual artefacts. 'Maybe you could point me in the right direction, to a suitable auction house?'

'No, it's not that. I've handled a great deal of china; I know one end of a Spode tureen from the other.' He grins, and I know he's not being sarcastic. Not that he ever would be; at least, I don't think so.

'But you're hesitating. If you'd rather not give me an opinion, that's cool.'

'Cool.' The eyebrows rise again, in amusement this time.

He's flirting with me. It's been a while — a very long while, discounting Jayden's friends who were mainly drunk, or worse, at the time — but I can still recognise flirting when I come across it. He has no right, and I have no right to enjoy it, which is what I am doing. I have to get him out of here, no two ways about it.

'I think,' Max says slowly, 'that if you're not in a hurry to sell then you should hang on to it a little longer.'

He turns towards the door of the sitting room.

Now I am annoyed. Is he an antique dealer, an expert in these things, or not?

'No, no. My mind's completely made up. I want to sell it now. Can you help me get it into auction or not?'

My brusqueness surprises him. He'd be even more surprised if he knew the reason for it.

'Okay. I'll tell you what I'll do.' He turns back to the table, picks up a cup and examines it again, all over, including the tell-tale gold Chelsea anchor. 'I'll take it off your hands myself, then you won't have to wait for the auction. How would that be?'

And then he names an amount which is pleasingly higher than I'd expected. From the bit of internet research I've managed to do in the local library — the cottage isn't connected yet — I've discovered that not only is Gran's tea set 1700s Chelsea, it's a rare design. The valuations on the internet came in at quite a bit higher than the figure Max is suggesting, but buying antiques and selling them are not the same thing, of course.

I pick up one of the cups myself,

appreciating again the depth of colour and the intricacy of the hand-painted pattern. Max hasn't said it's a rare design. In fact, he hasn't actually said anything about the china at all. But he's right, there's no point in hanging on for the right auction, and even if the set fetched more than Max is offering, I'd have to pay commission. I put the cup down, and smile.

'Well, thank you very much. I accept your offer.'

We shake hands rather formally, which makes me want to giggle, and we arrange a time and day for him to come and pick up the china. I see him to the door. As he steps outside, he hesitates and turns towards me, smiling uncertainly, as if he's not sure what comes next. There's a moment of awkwardness between us as I smile back, equally uncertainly. And then he ducks towards me and I lean in at the same time, arms just shy of a hug, air kisses just short of actual contact. It's only a moment, but it's enough for me to feel the warmth of him and catch a breath of aftershave or cologne, heavenly and expensive. It's these things I'm thinking about as I close the door and go back inside.

★   ★   ★

The members of my art class greet my floral offerings with their usual good-humoured enthusiasm. The enamel jug and some of Gran's old vases from the cottage come in handy as containers, and I arrange them down the centre of the table.

'They're pretty. Nice and cheerful for a grim day,' Lizzie says, positioning herself in front of the vase containing the roses. The others agree.

She's right about the weather. The clouds are racing past the windows, trailing grey shreds in their wake as the first drops of rain hit the glass. I make a mental note to pick up some logs for the fire from the garage on the way home.

After my demonstration on drawing flowers, everyone dives in, and then I remember to tell them about Olivia Morton coming to model for us. This news is greeted with the usual verve while I pretend not to notice Malcolm's lascivious wink towards the other men in the group. Hopefully there won't be any schoolboyish tittering when the time comes.

At tea break, as we stand about in the kitchen at the back of the hall, waiting for our turn at the kettle, the conversation turns to our favourite artists, and then drifts on to architecture. I casually mention Robin Hill.

'Ooh yes, wonderful house. Edwardian, isn't it?' Lizzie says, prising the lid off the sugar tin.

'I went to a garden party there once,' Marigold adds. 'A charity thing. I never managed a proper look inside, though, only through the window.' She chuckles. 'It was donkey's years ago, when the Parsons family lived there. They had two sets of twins, all girls. Packed them off to boarding school, and who can blame them?'

I jump in before they move on. 'I expect the house has changed a bit since then.'

'Mm? Yes, probably has,' Marigold says as we carry our drinks back to the table. 'I remember seeing new kitchen units going in when I was passing, just after the new owner moved in. He's an antique dealer. Looks of a movie star, and always very pleasant if you bump into him, but you've got to watch him. Oh yes, charm the birds off the trees, he would.' She gives a kind of sideways nod.

'Max Finch?' The name escapes before I have time to retract it.

'You've met him, then?' Lizzie gives me a look, her curiosity awakened.

'He introduced himself, yes. He is a neighbour, of course,' I say, trying not to give too much away.

'Well, it's nice you've got somebody handy.' Lizzie's tone suggests that this somehow makes up for his shortcomings, whatever they might be. 'You could feel a bit isolated otherwise.'

I hide a smile. Lizzie is fishing — not for the first time. She's wondering what I'm doing all alone in a cottage down a country lane, as I do myself sometimes, until I remember. I, in turn, am doing my own spot of fishing about Max Finch, but so far I've only caught a tiddler.

'I'm fine,' I say. 'I like living on my own.'

I'm not entirely sure this is true yet. It will take more time to find out.

'Yes, you do need to keep a sharp eye on that one.' Malcolm backtracks on the conversation, obviously having been listening in.

There are nods from around the table. While hands have been busy with pencils and watercolours, ears have been working overtime.

'So,' I say, keeping my eyes on the poppies I'm drawing, 'what do you mean exactly, about having to watch Max Finch?' I keep my tone conversational, as if this is just inconsequential gossip, which it is to them.

Malcolm puts down his brush. 'Well, since you ask, there was a bit of a hoo-hah last year when a woman tried to take him to court for swindling her elderly mother out of some antiques. *Plus*, that shop of his is hardly ever open. That's a sign of something dodgy if ever there was one.'

Malcolm taps the side of his nose.

'Shop? I didn't know we had an antique shop.'

'We haven't,' Marigold says. 'Max Finch's shop's in Little Barton, five miles up the road.' She lowers her glasses and peers at Malcolm over the top of them. 'How the devil do you know it's never open? You don't go to Little Barton.'

'That's all you know,' Malcolm says. 'I'm over there regular as clockwork. The missus likes their bakery.' Picking up his brush again, he dips it into his mug of tea instead of the water-pot. 'Drat!'

'They do a nice teacake at Little Barton,' says Marigold. 'I'll give you that.'

50

As the banter continues around me, wandering randomly across various topics, I think about my Chelsea china and my heart takes a dive. Of course Max will sell it on because that's his business, but perhaps what he's paying me isn't a fair sum after all. Oh, *please*, not more dubious dealings. Max has such an honest face and a winning way about him. But then so had Jayden. I decide I need to know more.

'What happened about the woman who tried to take Max Finch to court?'

Everyone speaks at once. They all have something to say, although their views seem to differ from one to the other; fact blending with fiction, by the sound of it. I sit there listening, the poppies neglected on the paper, and try to piece the story together.

I gather that the woman in question went to visit her mother one day to find several items missing, including a centuries-old, carved oak chest, a solid silver biscuit barrel and a couple of paintings. A 'charming man' had come to the door, the mother had explained. Earning himself entry by some solicitous chat, he'd proceeded to offer her fifty pounds for a rather ugly Victorian vase. Delighted at the sale, she'd then let him relieve her of the other things for less than the price of a bag of chips — this from Malcolm.

'Typical tactics of a knocker-boy,' Kevin, the man to the right of Malcolm, adds helpfully.

I know exactly what a knocker-boy is. Surely they aren't accusing Max of being one?

'It wasn't Max Finch himself who bought the things from the old lady,' Lizzie says. 'But the daughter did a bit of detective work and found out that the man who called worked for him, which kind of made Max responsible.'

'He got away with it.' Marigold nods around the group. 'His sort always do.'

Now I'm beginning to feel even more uncomfortable, and not only about the fate of my Chelsea china. At the same time, I can't help feeling annoyed about this blatant assassination of Max's character.

'Maybe there was nothing to get away *with*,' I say. 'If, as you say, he didn't call on the old lady in person, he might not have known anything about it.'

'Exactly what he said to the police,' Malcolm says. '*Plus*, there was no evidence — none that they found, anyway.'

'There you are, then.'

I put down my pencil, realising I've been chewing the end of it. But the doubts are already mushrooming in my mind, and I can't escape the meaningful glances that are passing from one to the other of my art group.

There's nothing I can do about the Chelsea tea-service now, but I can do something about Max Finch. I can keep well away from him in future, and not only because of his alleged underhanded business methods. The image of the sylph-like woman letting herself into his house is still clear in my mind.

*　*　*

My resolution to keep away from Max Finch lasts only until the following morning. I'm just about to set out for a painting session on Fold Hill when the landline phone rings and it's him. As I answer, I make a mental note to upgrade Gran's phone to one with caller display.

'Violet, tell me if I'm being too cheeky,' he begins, as my resolve starts to crumble at the sound of his voice, 'but you know a lot about art, don't you? Paintings, I mean. I gathered that from what you were saying the other day.'

I don't remember saying that exactly, but we talked about all sorts. When Max called for the china, which I'd carefully wrapped in kitchen paper and packed into an old crate I found under the stairs, I made tea; and, as it was a warm afternoon, we took it out into the back garden and sat in tattered deckchairs beside the gnarled old pear tree.

The conversation flowed easily and Max stayed for almost an hour. I kept my mind focused, making sure I didn't mention London, Brick Lane, or any part of my old life which might have brought questions I had no intention of answering.

Thinking about it later, I realised Max was playing the same kind of game, keeping to neutral topics, giving away little about his personal life. He did tell me he'd taken over the business from his father, having served a long apprenticeship with him. He also told me about some of his most interesting finds, some of which he'd picked up in the French *brocantes*, and we chatted generally about art, but not in any detail.

'I'm not any kind of expert,' I answer, carefully, 'but I've worked in a few galleries, and I like to think I have an eye for quality.'

'Exactly what I hoped you'd say,' Max says. I can imagine the light in those appealing brown eyes. 'Would you do me the biggest favour, Violet? Would you come with me to the auction preview and give me the benefit of your opinion?'

'I didn't think you dealt in paintings.'

'I don't, usually, but there's quite a collection coming up at my usual place and I may pick up the odd one. Besides, I thought it was time I did something about my entire ignorance of the art world.'

'Yes, I'll come if you think it would help. When is it?'

'Next Wednesday, a week tomorrow. I'm going away for a few days but I'll be in touch when I get back.'

'Oh, you're going away?'

Why did I say that? It's not as if I'm interested in Max's comings and goings, and even if I was, he doesn't need to know about it.

'Just down to Dorset. There's a country house sale I want to attend, and I'll take care of some other business while I'm about it.'

'Well, I hope it goes well,' I say. 'See you next week, then.'

* ⋆ ⋆

I decide to drive to Fold Hill rather than cycle, then I can do a supermarket shop on the way home. As I pass Robin Hill, I can't help wondering what Max is doing now. The little yellow sports car and the blue van are parked outside, so I know he's still in. Those are not the only vehicles. The grey estate car is there too, giving me a sharp — and timely — reminder that Max Finch is a friendly neighbour, one I happen to be doing a spot of business with, and nothing more.

Well, that's fine by me. In fact, it's definitely for the best. Occasionally, I get a spike of pain below my ribcage when I think about Jayden, and although I don't regret leaving, the overwhelming love I felt for him before it all changed hasn't vanished completely. Instead, it forms a kind of shadow which, when it passes over, darkens for a moment everything beneath it, like a cloud passing over fields.

Robin Hill is out of sight, hidden around the bend in the road, when it occurs to me how strange it is that I haven't met Max's wife, or girlfriend, whichever she is. But perhaps when he travels around, she goes with him, or she works somewhere away from the village and isn't around during the day. I expect it's only a matter of time before I bump into her, or Max introduces us.

My undisciplined mind is still on Max when I reach the crossroads. One of the signs points to Little Barton, and, telling myself I have all day to paint, I make the diversion. Before long, I'm bumping the car over the little humpback bridge which spans a narrow tributary of the river, and parking just off the high street. Like Fold, Little Barton is a typical quaint Sussex village, only smaller. The high street is a cosy jumble of cottages fronting onto the pavement, interspersed with shops, a black-and-white timbered pub, and an ugly red-brick Victorian village hall sprouting posters for various events, past and future. Like Fold again, passers-by nod and smile as I stroll along whilst trying not to seem as if I'm looking for something. This little expedition has a covert feel to it and I'd rather not be offered directions.

I pass the bakery, which must be the one Malcolm visits on behalf of his 'missus' — I can't see any other. The delicious aroma of baking drifts out of the half-open door and makes my mouth water. My appetite has certainly increased since I moved to the country; it must be all the fresh air. Perhaps I'll nip back and pick up something tasty to take up to Fold Hill. Now, though, I can see the object of my mission just ahead, on the other side of the road.

The logo above the shop-front is the same as on the van: *Maxwell Finch Antiques*. Remembering Malcolm's words, I laugh to myself as I see the 'Closed' sign on the glass door, and a phone number for enquiries. Not that I'd expected the shop to be open, as Max is at home at Robin Hill. Or, at least, he was. My eyes swivel from the darkened glass of the shop-front to the road, but there's no sign of him. Shading my eyes with both hands, I lean my forehead against the glass to peer inside. The window and what I can see of the shop behind it are packed with the usual assortment of antiques and curios. I gasp and jerk backwards as two bright eyes meet mine, then I'm laughing as I realise the eyes belong to a large stuffed owl perched on top of an old washstand.

I'm not sure what I'm doing here. I stand back from the window and think about this for a moment, and then I realise that I'm gathering information about Max Finch; it's as simple as that. I don't expect to find my precious Chelsea china sitting in the window. Although some of the things for sale look expensive, my tea-service probably wouldn't fetch the best price in a village antique shop. No, I'm here for the same reason I agreed to go to the auction preview. What's that saying, the one

Dad uses all the time? *Knowledge is power*. The more I know about my neighbourly antique dealer, the less likely I am to be taken in by him — in any respect.

★   ★   ★

From the top of Fold Hill, the panoramic view encompasses acres of chequered fields, punctuated by doll-sized buildings, and studded with woodland. The sheet of watercolour paper taped to the board has become a melting, impressionistic mix of greens and golds and tawny-brown, blending into a hardly-there blue wash for the sky. There's nothing like painting out of doors for capturing the spirit of a place, but I'm also happy working at the cottage where I've stripped the second bedroom of carpet and furnishings and turned it into a kind of studio. Ideally, I'd like more light than the two small sash windows give, but it's homely and peaceful and it suits my purpose.

A sharp little breeze suddenly arrives, flattening the grasses and sending a chill right through me. I'm wearing my usual paint-splodged jeans, but I've only got a T-shirt on top, so I take my red hooded fleece out of the rucksack and wriggle into it. The paper bag from the bakery at Little Barton comes out of the rucksack with it. I've been so absorbed in my painting that I'd forgotten about the apple Danish I bought earlier. The sugary top glistens where it's melted a bit in the bag, which makes it taste even more scrumptious.

Finishing the pastry, I wipe my sticky hands on the grass and take a swig from the water bottle; but instead of taking up the brush again, I lie back on the grass with my hands behind my head, gazing up at the wide, pale sky.

Next week is the first life class for my art group, and I'm already wondering if I've done the right thing in starting it up. If it doesn't go well, it will be down to me to explain to our model that we

don't need her any more. The commit-
tee in charge of the money side
wouldn't complain. I heard there were
raised eyebrows when I put in for the
ten pounds an hour I need to pay her,
but luckily it was granted in the end. I
could hardly ask her to strip off in a
draughty hall for less than the going
rate, could I? It's just as well we're not
in the depths of winter.

But it's too late to worry now.
Besides, there's no reason why it
shouldn't go well, providing Malcolm
and company behave themselves, which
I'm sure they will. I wonder what Olivia
Morton's like? Marigold described her
as 'young, but not too young to know
the difference', whatever that's supposed to mean. Malcolm said she had
good bone structure and was pretty
enough if you like them that thin. The
others — those who'd had the pleasure
before — seemed ambivalent about
who they were drawing and were more
concerned about *how*, as well they
might be. Life drawing is not for the

faint-hearted. I don't suppose it's a bundle of fun for the model either, although Olivia should be fine if she's as experienced as she claims.

It really is getting nippy now. The clouds are moving faster across a sky that's now more grey than blue. Sitting up, I begin to pack up my equipment, leaving the board with the painting on until the last minute to allow the paint to dry before I slide the whole thing into a plastic sack. I'll finish it at home, from memory and the photos I took before I started.

I avoid Little Barton as I drive home, but I pass Robin Hill again, and can't help noting that the van is still there while the yellow sports car and the grey estate are both missing. They've gone out separately, then, the two of them. I feel childishly pleased.

The post comes a lot later here than it did in London, and as I open my front door, it scuffs across a flurry of mail. Dumping my rucksack, I gather it up and take it through to the kitchen. I drop each envelope onto the table as I glance through. Credit card statement; something from the broadband people about getting me connected, at long last; a pretty postcard from Mum. The rest is junk.

One item, though, stands out from the junk mail. It's a long white envelope with my name and address on a printed label, and a real stamp. There's no company name, but I don't suppose it's anything important, and I wait until I've brought my painting stuff in from the car and switched the kettle on before I sit down at the table and open it.

At first there appears to be nothing inside, and then I ferret out a rough-edged slip of white paper — and the words I read, written untidily in black biro, cause me to reel back in shock.

You are not welcome in our village.
Go home.

Dropping the slip of paper as if it's red-hot, I bite my lower lip and look around the kitchen, then out of the window, then back at the blatant message. I realise my hands are shaking. *Who would do this?* Everyone in the village is so friendly and nice.

Well, not everyone, apparently. If this is genuine, somebody wants me gone, and they're deadly serious about it.

5

Max left Dorchester behind and set out on the A35, driving steadily, not too fast. He'd not had the best night's sleep. His stuffy room in the small hotel where he'd stayed for one night was painted forest green, with black beams across the low ceiling and dark furnishings, obviously intended to give atmosphere. All it had given Max was claustrophobia, especially when he'd tried to open the windows and found them painted shut.

Last night there'd been one heck of a lot of noise from the revelry in the bar directly below his room, which had kept him awake until gone midnight. This morning, feeling as if he'd had hardly any sleep at all, he'd woken gritty-eyed, headachy and out of kilter. In hindsight, he'd have been better off in the Travelodge, but it had seemed sensible at the time to book in somewhere close to the Georgian country house where the sale was. The hotel was only a stone's throw away, on the same road as the house.

However, there was more to Max's disturbed night than the noise and the feeling of entrapment. His own thoughts had also been responsible. It was always the same when he was due to see Sarah. One minute he'd be fine, and the next — *pow!* He'd be steamrollered by anxiety and wondering frantically what excuse he could make to cancel the visit. But then he'd have to rearrange, and so far he had never cancelled, not since she'd been admitted to Maytree Grange. Besides, it wasn't Sarah's fault she'd got ill, and Maytree Grange was on his route home. So, no excuses.

He'd had a good day at the sale, and picked up a number of items which were now safely stowed in the back of the van. Attending the auction had reminded him of his forthcoming date with Violet. Okay, it wasn't a date as such, and most likely she'd be bored rigid looking over a load of old stuff in what was no more than a glorified shed, but that was a chance he'd have to take.

He'd been attracted to her right from that first day when he'd gone into the field where she'd been painting and introduced himself. And unless he'd forgotten all he'd ever known about women and their body language, she'd felt the same about him. She'd been wearing paint-spattered jeans and a red hoodie which, with her soft, corn-coloured hair falling out of its ponytail, made her look like a teenager. Except she wasn't, of course, and once he'd got close up, her womanliness and the undisguised directness of her blue-eyed gaze as she appraised him had sent his pulse racing.

Violet Brooke. He'd been curious. More than curious. Crazy to know more about her. He wished now that he'd known the other Violet, her grandmother, but although he'd racked his brains, all he could conjure up was a vague impression of a little old lady tending the garden of Sunrise Cottage as he swung past in the car or the van.

Against his better judgement, and having learned virtually nothing from the chat in the pub and shops in Fold other than that Violet was teaching art at the village hall, he'd resorted to the internet. And there, looking a little different from the way she did now, but unmistakeable, was Violet Brooke, pictured outside a club or restaurant on the arm of some young arty upstart called Jayden Fox. Another picture showed a hazy glimpse of her behind the wheel of a Toyota — the same car she had now — with Jayden in the passenger seat. Lastly, there was a blurry shot of her on the balcony of what looked like a very trendy block of flats. These pictures were printed alongside images of Jayden himself, as juicy little embellishments to the main story.

The official report of the case said he'd had no idea that the wild, vibrant paintings which were so evocative of their original creator, a Spanish artist, were intended to be auctioned as being by the artist himself. Fox had painted those works, not as forgeries but as upfront copies. The real culprits, Max read, were a group of hangers-on who'd professed to be his friends. But some of the reporting had a definite slant towards doubting Fox's version of events. He must have had a damn good lawyer, Max had thought, as he'd ploughed through the internet articles.

The press interest in Violet, it seemed, wasn't really about her at all. It was just a way of filling out the detail of Jayden Fox's life. Some articles referred to her as his girlfriend, others as his fiancée. Under the circumstances, he couldn't blame her for leaving London and burying herself down here. Clearly she hadn't enjoyed her moment of reflected fame. She'd left Jayden, that much was obvious, but just as obvious was that she'd come to Sussex for a new start, and he mustn't go barging in and asking her about her past. He wasn't that insensitive. If she wanted to tell him, she would do so in her own good time.

One thing was certain, though. He couldn't stay away. He felt ashamed that he'd asked her to come to the auction viewing with him purely as an excuse to spend time with her; he had no intention of buying any paintings. But not so ashamed that he wasn't going to go through with it.

Sweet Violet. That was how Max thought of her, which was often.

★   ★   ★

Maytree Grange was set in parkland on a road just outside Petersfield. Sheep bleated from the meadow and wandered, oblivious, across the long, winding drive as Max drove slowly towards the imposing Elizabethan mansion. When Sarah needed residential care, which increasingly she did, Maytree Grange was the best. Her parents paid for it, and how lucky it was that they could afford it.

Bringing the van to rest at a discreet distance from the ground-floor windows, Max saw one half of the huge oak front door swing open. Kathy, one of Sarah's regular carers, must have seen him approach. She smiled as he stepped into the cool, wood-panelled hall which smelt of beeswax and roses.

'Mrs Finch is outside, on the patio. She'll be made up to see you.'

Sarah would always be Mrs Finch to Kathy, even though technically speaking, she wasn't any more.

'Thank you. I'll go on through.'

'You do that. I'll organise some tea.'

As soon as he entered the hushed elegance of the lounge, Max caught sight of Sarah through the French doors. She was sitting in a white wicker chair, reading a book, leaning back so that her long dark hair trailed over the back of the chair. The flower-print cotton dress she was wearing was draped over her outstretched legs, almost reaching her ankles. A purple fringed shawl was thrown around her thin shoulders. Max's breathing stalled as for a moment he saw the old Sarah, the girl he'd married after a whirlwind three-month love affair when he was just twenty-two, and Sarah three years older. His hippy-happy girl, as he'd liked to call her. That was before it all went wrong.

'Hey,' she said, as Max went up to her and dropped a kiss on her pale cheek. 'I wondered how long it'd be before you showed up again.'

Her face was serious, eyes accusing. Ignoring the implied criticism, knowing it wasn't truly meant, Max pulled up a chair and sat down.

'I was on my way back from a sale. Thought I'd stop by. How are you?'

She gave a little mirthless laugh. 'I'm here, aren't I? Not at home in my little flat. That must tell you something.'

Max sighed inwardly. This could be one of those times when nothing he said, or did, would be right. There'd been plenty of times like that, down the years. Reminding himself that it wasn't Sarah's fault she was unwell, he found a smile.

'I know, I'm sorry. I just meant, how are you feeling today?'

Sarah laid her book down on the ground and hitched herself upright in the chair.

'I'm so tired all the time. They say it's the meds, but I'm not sure because I was just as tired when I stopped taking them.'

Ah, he'd thought as much. She'd stopped the tablets, which naturally had brought on one of her episodes and landed her back in here. But there was no point in referring to it or trying to rationalise. Instead he told her about the country house sale, and as they chatted about inconsequential things, Sarah began to smile and the light returned to her eyes.

'We were good once, you and me,' she said, after a short pause in the conversation.

'We were. We had some great times.'

Sarah looked down at her hands, twisting them in her lap, then looked up again.

'I do like you, Max, but I don't love you any more and you don't love me, not in that way. That's how it is, isn't it?'

'Yep, that's how it is.'

Sarah gave a big sigh, as if this was news to her, and a great relief. 'Good. I'm glad you see it the same way as me. You do, don't you?'

Max nodded. She did this all the time, kept going over the same old ground. But if it helped her to sort out the muddles in her mind, what did it matter?

'I don't know what to do with it. The decree thingy. It is silly of me not to know, isn't it?'

'No, love, it's not silly at all. It's not like we've done it before. Just keep it where you keep all your other paper-work. That's all.'

'Oh yes, you said that last time.' She

smiled weakly. 'I'm sorry I keep asking you the same thing, only I'm just so tired.'

'I know, it's fine.'

Seeing one of the male carers coming towards them with the tea-tray, Max got up and fetched a small round table from the corner of the patio. He was glad of the diversion.

When they were settled again and the tea poured, Max broached the subject that had been playing on his mind.

'The house,' he said, helping himself to a ginger biscuit. 'Robin Hill . . . '

'Yes, I know what's it called,' Sarah said. 'I haven't lost every last marble yet. What about the house?'

'I want you to have the lion's share of it. Three-quarters at least. My name might be on the deeds, but we wouldn't have been able to afford it if your parents hadn't given us a huge chunk towards it, so it's only fair. Presuming you don't want to move back in, we need to have a conversation about selling it at some point. When you're back on your feet, of course.'

Sarah shook her head, smiling indulgently at him. So she did remember.

'You're so hopeless, Maxy. I've already said I don't want a penny out of the house. You love it there, it's your home, and you mustn't think of selling it. If you like we can arrange to transfer the deeds so it's entirely in your name. For God's sake, Max, it's the least I can do, with all you've had to put up with.'

'That cuts two ways,' he said. 'I wasn't the easiest to live with, we both know that. We had some right royal rows, and a lot of them were down to me.'

Sarah tapped her temple. 'But you had all my weird stuff to cope with; and I know that wasn't my fault, but you didn't run away from that, did you? Not like some men would. Anyway, my parents are rich, remember? They've bought me my flat in Worthing, my sister's round the corner, I've got friends and I'm happy there. So you just enjoy Robin Hill and your pokey little village in the arse-end of nowhere, and let that be an end to it.'

Max couldn't help laughing. Never in a million years would he let Sarah make the house over to him. At the very least she should keep her half-share, but there was no point in arguing the toss now. Still, it was a relief to know he could go on living at Robin Hill for the time being, even though that knowledge came with a large dose of guilt.

'Well, perhaps we'll talk about it another time,' he said.

'If we must.' She smiled, the old Sarah shining through. 'You're lovely, you know that? You're not for me, but you're a good man, and it's time you found somebody else. Go and get yourself a girlfriend, a new wife, whatever.'

Max grinned. 'I might just do that.'

It had been a good visit, the best he could have hoped for. Not only because of Sarah's sweet generosity about the house, but because she was talking and making sense, and not getting angry. It wasn't always that way, after one of her episodes. It was all so unpredictable. But seeing her almost cheerful today made his heart lift. Their marriage may have been over years ago, in theory and now in practice, but he still cared about her.

If he and Violet became close — as close as he dared hope they would be — he would tell her about Sarah, of course. There was no rush, though. A bloke with an ex-wife on the scene, even if there were exceptional circumstances, wasn't exactly an attractive prospect. He couldn't imagine Violet having a jealous bone in her body, but he couldn't say for sure. He hardly knew her, which was something he planned to remedy as soon as possible.

6

My art class behaves very well at our first life session, even Malcolm. For all their joshing, they rise to the challenge, and for a change the hall actually falls silent for long spells at a time. Rather than sitting at the table, I've got everyone on chairs in a rough semi-circle, with drawing boards on their knees. We're just drawing today, some with pencil, some with charcoal. Paints will come out on another day, but I decide to keep it simple for this first session.

I circulate, quietly giving guidance about proportions and perspective and light and shade, and in between I work on my own drawing — which, I have to admit, is not one of my better efforts. There's a reason for this. I'm in a state of shock . . . well, sort of.

When Olivia Morton sashayed through

the door earlier, I recognised her immediately as the woman I'd seen going into Max's house. I must have come across as a bumbling idiot as I welcomed her, and I saw her perfectly shaped eyebrows raise a touch as I shook her hand rather overenthusiastically in my attempt to behave normally. My curiosity was at an all-time high, but there was no time to make idle chat, and I forced all thoughts of Max Finch from my mind as my students began to arrive.

I'd purloined an old screen from one of the side rooms and stood it in the corner of the hall for our model to change behind. I found myself holding my breath as she emerged, wearing a luxurious white towelling dressing gown with a discreet hotel logo on the pocket, but Olivia's obvious ease in this situation somehow calmed me down. Dropping the dressing gown onto the floor as if it was an old rag, she'd arranged herself on a red velvet sofa I borrowed from the drama group's prop room, and I could tell straight away that she was, as she'd promised, a professional at sitting.

I'm concentrating hard, both on my own drawing and those of my students, but it's a weird feeling, being in the same room as Max's wife/girlfriend, especially when she's stark naked. I'd imagined the likely scenarios of my first meeting with this woman, but never this. My pencil wobbles in my hand as my mind becomes a kaleidoscope of mixed emotions, and I realise how much I've let Max get under my skin.

Talking of skin, Olivia's, naturally, is smooth and completely unblemished — all over. I bet she uses really expensive creams on it every day, or perhaps she just got lucky with the genes and has to make no effort at all. She has incredible bone structure, which doesn't apply solely to her face, and her ultra-slim body is toned to perfection so that she looks healthy and not skinny. I remember the sports bag she had when I saw her at Robin Hill. I expect she'd just come from the gym.

We're due a break shortly, and I'm hoping I'll have the chance to chat to her and sneak in a few pertinent questions. My motives aren't exactly as pure white as that dressing gown, but my stupid attraction to Max needs to be put in its place, and getting to know Olivia will surely help that along.

Her eyes are incredibly lovely as well as the rest of her, I'm thinking, as I adjust their cat-like shape on my drawing and lightly pencil in some shadow at the corners. Kevin's waving his pencil politely in my direction, and I get up and go over.

'Do I put in that bit, you know, down there?' He pulls a face and shyly jabs his pencil in a southerly direction.

I have to laugh to myself. Kevin is a retired police officer, upright and confident. He's seen it all, one way or another, yet here he is, obviously embarrassed about pencilling in the dark triangle visible from his view of Olivia.

Marigold, next to Kevin, answers for

me, without lowering her voice.

'Of course put it in! No good being lily-livered about it.'

I look up in time to see Olivia's lips twitch in amusement. The light moment helps me relax, and I decide to make one more round of my hardworking students before we break for tea.

Marigold is pretty good at life drawing, easily the best in the group. She's drawn Olivia and other models before, and clearly has a natural talent. Moving round the group, the levels of ability and the styles they use vary widely, but Olivia Morton springs to life in some form or another on every board. Everyone seems contented and absorbed, and I'm pleased it's all going so well.

I clap my hands like a nursery school teacher, and announce tea break. Drawing boards thump to the wooden floor as my lot make the dash to be first at the kettle and the biscuit tin. Olivia stays put, elegantly draping one arm over the edge of the sofa and gazing unseeingly out of the top window as if she's got something on her mind. She seems distant, preoccupied, and I feel suddenly shy of her.

'Would you like some tea, or coffee?' I ask. 'If you want to slip your dressing gown on and come over. Or I'll bring you one back, if you like.'

Olivia seems to gather herself, swinging her legs and standing up in one smooth movement. Again, I'm a little bit fazed by her nakedness so close to me, which I've never been with the other models I've worked with, but I'm sure I'll get over that in time.

She picks up the robe and flings it on, tying the belt, before she replies.

'No, thanks. I never drink tea or coffee. I brought water with me.'

She smiles brightly, but there's a brittle feel about it that puzzles me, and I wonder if she's not used to such basic surroundings for her modelling work. But then I think it can't be that, because she's done this before in this very hall.

'Oh, okay then. Breaks usually last about fifteen minutes. I'll leave you to it.'

'I'm just popping out to my car,' Olivia says. 'I've left my phone and I need to call Maria. She's my childminder.'

Childminder? If I thought I'd had my share of surprises this morning, I was wrong.

'Yes, do, of course.'

Olivia must have seen my confusion. 'I have a daughter, Anna. She's two-and-a-half. She goes to Maria most days. Won't be a tick.'

Olivia swings out of the door, barefoot and wearing nothing but a dressing gown. I can't help going to the side window and peering out, in time to see her getting into the grey estate car which is, fortunately, parked on the small forecourt close to the building and not out in the street, although I have the impression that wouldn't bother her.

My head is spinning as I cross the

hall and enter the crowded kitchen area, bumping into Lizzie coming out with her mug of tea.

'All right?' she says, giving me an odd look.

'I'm not sure. Lizzie, can I ask you something?'

She pulls me to one side, away from the kitchen entrance. 'What's that, then?'

I decide to come right out with it, and never mind what Lizzie thinks.

'Is Olivia Max Finch's wife?'

Lizzie seems taken aback for a second. 'Max's *wife*? Good gracious, no. Whatever gave you that idea?'

'His girlfriend, then?'

'Well, in *theory* I suppose there could be something going on there; but she doesn't live with him, I can tell you that for certain.'

I feel a bolt of relief. 'Where does she live, then?'

Lizzie waves a vague hand. 'Somewhere between here and Little Barton, I believe.'

'She's got a little girl, she just told me that.'

'She's a single mother; well, that's what I heard. She doesn't let much go about her private life, so don't take that as gospel.'

'Take what as gospel?' Malcolm comes up to us, not wanting to miss anything.

Lizzie glances at me. 'Violet thought Olivia was married to Max Finch,' she says, returning to my original question.

'I didn't *think* it exactly. It just crossed my mind, that's all.' I wish I hadn't started this now.

Malcolm turns to Lizzie. 'I don't think she's married to anyone, is she?'

'That's what I said.'

'*Plus*,' says Malcolm, 'She hasn't got a ring on.'

'That doesn't prove a thing . . . '

Lizzie and Malcolm are in a gossipy huddle now, leaving me out of it, which is a relief. They're still at it when Olivia comes back and trips lightly across the floorboards to resume her pose on the sofa. Shushing the pair of them, I smile across at Olivia, indicating we're ready to go again.

Back at my drawing board, I flick my pencil over the paper, scrutinising Olivia with what I hope looks like a professional eye while I mentally tick off the facts. Olivia and Max aren't married. She has a child. She doesn't live at Robin Hill, at least not all the time. And that, for what it's worth, is all I've managed to gather. But Lizzie's throwaway comment that there could be something going on between Max and Olivia is more than enough to stop me making a total fool of myself when I go to the auction viewing tomorrow.

★   ★   ★

When the class is over and everyone's left, including Olivia, I take my time tidying up. My students are pretty good at clearing up after themselves, but a couple of chairs still remain out in the middle of the hall, and a trail of pencil shavings litters the floor. I fetch the dustpan and brush from the kitchen and deal with those, and only when I'm satisfied everything's clean and tidy, ready for the WI meeting this afternoon, do I gather my things together and lock the door after me.

The keys have to be returned to Mrs Leaver, who acts as the hall caretaker among her other numerous village duties, and after I've put my things in the car, I nip along the street to her whitewashed cottage and post them through her letterbox. Then I pick up some bread, ham and salad from the mini-supermarket before I drive home.

It's as I'm approaching the first bend in Clayfoot Lane that I realise who is behind me. I recognise the car first as I glance in the rear-view mirror, and then its driver — Olivia Morton. She's close enough to realise it's me, but she doesn't acknowledge me in any way as I signal left and pull into the side outside my cottage. No toot or wave or anything. So maybe she didn't spot me after all.

But what's she doing along here in the first place? My mind conjures up only two possibilities. Either she's going home, to wherever she lives on the way to Little Barton, having collected her daughter from the childminder, or she's heading straight to Robin Hill for a cosy lunch with Max, followed by an even cosier afternoon. Do I care which it is? Stupidly, I do.

* * *

So far I've managed to push out of my mind the threatening note I received, but while I'm sitting by the window, watching for Max to arrive, I see the corner of it poking out from under Gran's clock on the mantelpiece. Why I didn't throw it away at the time, I have no idea; but I didn't, and now I'm wondering if I should tell somebody about it. *But who?* is the question. On the other hand, perhaps I should chuck it out now and forget about it. I do think I overreacted when it first arrived.

It was probably from one of the village's more eccentric characters — a fruit-loop, as Dad would say — or it was a complete mistake and it wasn't intended for me at all.

But I don't get as far as throwing it away, because I hear a toot from beyond the hedge, and moments later Max comes through the gate. My front garden is very small and it only takes him a couple of strides along the brick path to reach the front door, so he's there by the time I open it.

'You look very nice,' he says, giving me an appreciative up-and-down glance which reminds me of the first time we met.

I sense he's slightly embarrassed by his own compliment as he rubs a hand across his head and glances momentarily away.

'Thanks.' I smile, and Max smiles back, right into my eyes, having made a super-quick recovery from his awkwardness.

I've put on a dress today instead of

my usual jeans or cut-offs — a summery, yellow-print dress which comes well above my knees. I'm wearing red strappy sandals, and my hair is freshly washed and falls loosely about my shoulders. I can't help feeling pleased that Max has noticed my efforts. He's looking pretty good himself. He's wearing immaculate pale-grey chinos and a slim-fitting navy-blue polo shirt. I realise how much I've missed seeing him this past week.

I'm surprised Max has brought the car — I'd expected the van as this is a business trip — but whizzing along the country lanes in a nippy yellow sports car gives the outing an extra frisson, and I sit back and enjoy the ride.

The auction house is around ten miles from Fold, on the edge of a sprawling village I haven't been to before. It's a quiet morning on the roads, so it's not long before we're pulling onto rough ground alongside a long, lofty building that looks as if it's been cobbled together out of a row of barns. There are only another couple of cars parked outside and very few people about as Max pushes open one of the double doors and stands back to allow me through first.

I'd expected the place to be buzzing, but the only auctions and viewings I've been to before were in and around London, and this is altogether different. I follow Max along the narrow aisles between the display goods with lot numbers stuck on.

'Don't be fooled,' he says, stopping to turn round to me. 'It may look like a load of old junk, which some of it is, but this place has a good reputation and there's usually a fair amount of competition for the finer pieces.' He leads me towards a small oak table with delicately turned legs and a wavy, decorative front. 'This, for example, is Georgian, eighteen-fifty. There's a reserve on it of five hundred.'

'I'm not surprised,' I say casually.

I don't want Max to think I'm a complete novice. I might well be in terms of country auctions, but I'm used to the eye-wateringly high price-tags on some of the stuff which Jayden and I saw in Brick Lane and other London markets.

Sadness clutches at my insides as I remember our beautiful Chinese red lacquered cabinet, hand-painted with little figures and rustic scenes. It was called a wedding cabinet — ironic, as that was where I left my engagement ring. I blink as a stray tear threatens. It sometimes happens like this: I think I'm all over Jayden, and then some small thing pierces a reminder through my heart.

'Violet, are you okay? It is a bit stuffy in here.' Max, who has walked on down the aisle, marking off his catalogue as he goes, realises I'm not behind him and comes back.

'I'm fine,' I say, gathering myself and offering a smile. 'So where are these paintings, then?'

Max hesitates for a second, as if he's no idea what I'm talking about. Then he says, 'Ah, yes, paintings. Right. They'll be up there.'

He points up towards a railed balcony that runs round three sides of the sale room.

'To be honest,' I say, giving no more than a cursory glance through the paintings in Lot 404, 'these aren't that desirable. They're Victorian, an unknown artist, and not that well painted.'

The pink-frocked child playing with a kitten is the worst, the others in the set — Pekingese lap-dogs on cushions; a woman in a shawl, clutching a rose and gazing woodenly out to sea — are not much better.

'I'll steer clear of those, then.' Max gives a little laugh.

I sift through similar offerings until eventually I come across a pair of small watercolour landscapes by a little-known but collectable artist.

'These might be a good buy, but I wouldn't pay more than forty for the pair.'

I hand one of the gold-framed

paintings to Max.

'I like them,' he says, turning the painting this way and that. 'If they don't sell I can always hang them up at home. That's the beauty of having a house like mine. Plenty of room for the stuff I accumulate in the line of duty.'

He seems thoughtful for a moment, before he smiles brightly.

'That's it, then.'

'That's it?'

'Well, yes. Sorry, you must be wondering what you're doing here, but I thought some of these lots would be larger, more for you to get your teeth into.'

'Did you?'

I don't know why he thought that. Looking over his shoulder at the catalogue, the lots are clearly described with the numbers of items included in each. Max doesn't answer, but hurries on back down the stairs.

There's no sign of my Chelsea here today. I've seen bench-loads of porcelain and pottery, the best items locked inside glass cases, and it definitely wasn't there. Of course, I knew it wouldn't be. What it fetches when Max sells it on is nothing to do with me, and presumably he wouldn't want me to know about it, especially if he's underpaid me. I do trust Max, at least I think I do, but I haven't forgotten the rumours I heard from my art group, and I wish I could be sure I haven't been duped.

Max spots somebody he knows across the other side of the sale room and says he'll be back in a minute. I take the opportunity to go to the hatchway behind which sits a spectacled woman in an untidy office.

'Is there a catalogue for the next sale — I mean, the one after this?'

'Not yet, dear. The next sale's not for a few weeks, towards the end of May,' she says. 'Do you want me to take your name and send you one when it's out? It'll cost you six pounds plus postage.'

I glance across and see Max heading back towards me.

'No, that's fine. I'll pop by and get one. Thank you.'

★ ★ ★

'Let's stop off at a pub and I'll buy you lunch. It's the least I can do,' Max says, as the car bumps over the stony parking area and back onto the road.

'You don't need to do that. I didn't do a lot, did I?'

'I know not to waste my money on Victorian sentimental subjects.' Max laughs. 'Violet, you were a great help.'

I hesitate. There's nothing I'd like better right now than lunch in a country pub with Max, which means I should politely decline and ask him to drop me home as soon as possible.

'It's just lunch,' he says, glancing at me.

Max has an uncanny knack of reading my mind, and I'm not sure how I feel about it.

'I know.'

I hesitate again, and suddenly I

wonder why I'm making this into something it clearly isn't. Max isn't single, I've firmly convinced myself of that. He's just being friendly and he has no ulterior motive. Why do I have to complicate everything?

'Yes, thanks, that would be lovely,' I say. 'Ooh, look, how about there? We could sit in the garden.'

We're passing the prettiest pub imaginable, called The Tinker's Rest. It has a cosy thatched roof, baskets of flowers hanging all the way along its white walls, and it's surrounded by a gorgeous cottage-style garden with tables and benches set out on the lawn. Max stops the car almost before my words are out.

'Perfect,' he says.

'Now, *this*,' I say a while later, as I'm sipping a frosty glass of white wine, 'is what I moved to Sussex for.'

'The wine?' Max grins cheekily, his eyes sparkling with amusement.

I grin back and raise my eyes. 'No, not the wine. Places like this.' I wave an encompassing arm. 'It's so sweet.'

'*Sweet.*'

He's making fun of me again. Flirting.

'You know what I mean.'

We're seated at a table in a sheltered spot beside a hedge, but despite the bright sun, it's a bit chilly for eating outside. I give a little shiver and Max notices.

'Shall we go inside? Or I've got a sweater in the boot. I could fetch it for you?'

'No, honestly, I'm fine.'

Our food arrives, and I'm wishing I'd ordered something hot instead of a prawn sandwich, but it's delicious, and so much tastier for being eaten out of doors. I say so to Max. He answers with a smile, a smile that reaches parts of me it has no business to be. Too late, I realise I'm a tiny bit drunk. I was woken up early by a cacophony of birdsong and had breakfast before seven. This wine — a large glass — is hitting a virtually empty stomach, and the sandwich has come too late to make any impression. Max has a Saint Clement's with his beef sandwich, and I feel suddenly guilty, though again this is the wine talking.

'I'm so *sorry*, Max,' I say. 'I feel dead mean, drinking alone.'

'Oh, Violet,' Max says, shaking his head slowly.

'What?'

'Oh, I don't know.' He laughs. 'You're funny, that's all.'

'Well, as long as it's in a good way.'

'Oh, yes. Definitely in a good way.' He widens his eyes just a smidgeon.

I want to ask Max to stop flirting with me. I want to ask him to stop smiling at me in that sort of private way. And I want to ask him to move his legs, which aren't quite touching mine but are so close I swear I can feel warmth from them.

But I don't do any of these things. Instead, I push the glass away while it still has some wine in it, and finish off the rest of my sandwich. And, while I'm about it, I give myself a stern internal talking-to. I haven't escaped my London life, and Jayden, only to fall in love with the first man I meet. I don't want that; my emotions won't stand any further pummelling. I want a quiet time, space to recover and take stock, and then I'll decide where my life's going next.

While I've been deep in thought, I haven't noticed Max reach across the table, and before I know it, he's placed his hand over mine. There's nothing I can do about it without seeming rude, and my heart gives a little skip.

'Violet,' Max says, 'tell me to mind my own business, but have you been hurt? Recently, I mean?'

'How d'you work that out?'

I didn't mean to snap, but I'm shocked at his question, and wonder where it's come from. Am I wearing a label on my forehead or something?

'I'm sorry,' Max says gently. 'That's a bit personal, I know. But I couldn't help noticing . . . '

He moves his hand away from mine

and glances down, and I see what Max sees, something that strangely enough I haven't noticed before: a faint white line across the third finger of my left hand. Where my engagement ring used to be.

'You're very observant.' I draw my hand back, away from his gaze.

Max waits silently for whatever I might be going to say next. Or not say. I sense he'd be fine either way, which makes me want to give him a little bit more.

I sigh, and reach for my glass to finish off the wine. Suddenly, I need it.

'Okay, yes, there was somebody, and we were engaged. It didn't work out, that's all. I was the one who ended it, but that doesn't make it any easier.'

Max's question has forced an image into my mind, one I've tried so hard to dispel these last few months. And it's nothing to do with Jayden's near-miss prosecution for forgery, nor the way he left me feeling unguarded and vulnerable in the face of the sensation-seeking press.

If I close my eyes, which I do now for a second, I can see Angelica, an artist who goes under the one name only — I always thought that pretentious — sitting with Jayden on the chaise longue in his studio. In our apartment. There's scarcely room for a cigarette paper between them. Jayden is looking extremely guilty, and shocked to see me there. Clearly neither of them heard me come in. Or maybe she did, because she doesn't look guilty at all. In fact, she looks triumphant.

I had no evidence of anything going on between them — Jayden's words when I challenged him later. But I know what I saw — or what I might have seen, had I arrived a few minutes earlier.

So yes, evidence or not, I have been hurt in precisely the way Max is probably thinking. Betrayed in love — such a cliché. As for the rest, he couldn't begin to guess at that, so I have the chance of retaining some privacy at least.

'If you ever need somebody to talk

to,' Max says, 'I'm a good listener. That's all I was going to say.'

'Thank you, but I'm fine. Or I will be.'

★ ★ ★

We don't talk much on the way back to Fold, but it's an easy silence. Back at Sunrise Cottage, Max unnecessarily gets out of the car and comes to the front door with me. He waits while I get my key out, and I wonder if he wants me to ask him in. There's a tiny awkward pause while I fumble with the key, which seems to have taken on a life of its own. Eventually I manage to wiggle it into the lock and open the door.

'Well, I'd better get going,' Max says, not moving.

There's a hint of regret in his voice. Or I could be imagining that.

'Violet, will I see you soon?' he says. He glances down at the ground, then back at me. 'I know it's early days for you, so tell me to sod off if you like, but I'd very much like to take you out to dinner some time. As friends, if that's how you prefer it.'

The smile he gives me, kind of shy but direct at the same time, tells me he definitely wants to be more than friends, and once again my stupid heart responds with a leap.

And then I remember.

'Max, aren't you forgetting something? Or, rather, some*one*?'

'How d'you mean?' He looks genuinely puzzled.

'I met Olivia. She came to do some modelling for my art group. *Nude* modelling.'

'Ah yes, she's done that before, I believe.'

We're missing the point here. I raise my eyes in impatience, wishing Max had zoomed off in that little yellow car and we'd missed out this conversation entirely.

'No, what I mean is,' I begin, making this as plain as I can because clearly I need to do that, 'what I mean *is*, you're hardly in a position to go around asking out other women, are you? Now, if you don't mind, I need to go in. I've got things to do.'

'Hey!' The astonishment in Max's eyes halts me in my tracks. 'What've I said? Why are you talking about my housekeeper?'

'Your *housekeeper*?'

Max smiles, my confusion seeming to amuse him. 'Yes, Olivia Morton. My housekeeper. Oh God, you didn't think she and I . . . ?' He gives a little laugh.

I feel idiotic, and ridiculously pleased at the same time. But I also feel a kind of pulling-in feeling, like the raising of a drawbridge, as the need to protect myself comes rushing in fast, stopping me making a mammoth mistake.

I shrug. 'I saw her going into your house. She's very beautiful. Why wouldn't you be together?'

'Because we're not, that's why. Never have been, never will be.' Max moves closer to me, raising his arms in an open, friendly gesture. 'Violet, can I give you a hug?'

'What for?'

'Because I want to.'

A challenging look comes my way, but it's not a serious one. I can't help laughing, hardly able to believe he's actually asked that.

'Go on, then.'

I step towards him and his arms encircle me. Mine creep around his back as I hold him, more tentatively than he's holding me. We stand there for a long moment, and then he gives a little sigh, raises his head from my shoulder, and before I know it his mouth is searching for mine.

'No.' I pull back, just in time. Max steps back and drops his arms to his side. 'I'm sorry, but I can't do this. You're right, it is early days for me. Not only that, I'm only here for the summer. I'll be gone in a few months. If I got involved with anyone — with you — it wouldn't be fair on either of us.'

Max says nothing. I watch him back

away and walk along the path, and when he reaches the gate he turns, presses a finger to his lips, then holds it out to me.

7

Finally, after three months of wrangling and broken promises, Sunrise Cottage has a viable internet connection, one that stays with me instead of failing every five minutes. The first thing I do, once I've checked that my old email address has definitely disappeared — just in case Jayden's got his act together and thought he might contact me that way — is to look up the next sale at the auction house I went to with Max. It's next week, so the catalogue will be out now. I make a mental note to drive over and pick one up. At the same time, I wonder why I'm bothering. I hardly think Max would have underpaid me for the Chelsea, then made a move on me.

But my time with Jayden has taken its toll, and I'm beginning to wonder if I'll ever trust anyone again. That's hardly fair on Max, but I can't help it. I need peace of mind more than anything. I check on other auctions in the vicinity, then those further afield, and order a couple of catalogues online. If those don't bear fruit, I'll let it go. There are more important things in life.

As spring gives way to summer, I'm loving Sunrise Cottage even more. Every day I take time to inspect the garden and see what's new. When I moved in, it was such a tangle that I expected to come across Sleeping Beauty at any moment — my fault for neglecting it for so long. But it was winter, and I left it to its own devices. When the weather warmed up, I cut the grass and tackled the most overgrown parts haphazardly, without really knowing what I was doing.

Yet somehow the garden has survived my inexpert attentions, and now tall spikes of hollyhocks and foxgloves embellish the front wall of the cottage, their tight buds showing hints of colour to come. The rest of the small front garden is a tapestry of pink and blue hardy geraniums, clumps of thrift, and cushions of tiny mauve and yellow flowers which cascade over the low front wall. More hollyhocks and foxgloves have sprung up randomly along each side of the back garden path. Roses ramble up the walls and over the privy-shed at the bottom of the garden. In a few weeks, there will be poppies and marigolds and stocks; all Granny Violet's favourite flowers, happily self-seeding against a backdrop of rampant ivy and honeysuckle.

The garden was the thing I loved most about the cottage as a child, especially on hot days when the scents were deliciously potent and the bees burrowed deep among the petals. I would climb up and sit on the lowest bough of the pear tree whilst I made up stories in my head about the fairies and elves who lived in the garden, invisible to everyone but me.

Remembering this brings a whisper of sadness, but it's soon gone as I hear Gran's kind, no-nonsense voice inside my head. No made-up fairy folk for her. Granny Violet was pragmatic and down-to-earth, and sometimes I wish I was more like her. Perhaps I am, in a way. Sometimes I look around Sunrise Cottage and wonder what on earth I think I'm doing, burying myself away in rural Sussex while London with all its vibrancy and potential rushes on without me. Then I think about that snowy day in February, my flight from the desolate apartment and my fragmented relationship with Jayden. A dreamer I may be, but I'm practical where it counts, and quite strong, I think. I suspect I'll need some of that strength to keep Max Finch at arm's length.

As the days drift away, so do my funds. My savings are dwindling fast. Apart from the village art class and the Saturday art club at the school, I've no regular income, and I haven't got round to looking for a job. The money Max paid me for the china was useful, but my intentions to sell some more of

Gran's things have come to nothing. This isn't entirely due to laziness; I've got used to having certain things around. I enjoy seeing them, especially the violet-themed items, like the framed embroidered pictures of the flowers, the beautifully-made wooden needlework box with violets painted on the lid, and the silver-backed dressing table set engraved with them. I don't want to part with any of these, and they wouldn't fetch much anyway.

I'm working hard on my painting, and have built up quite a collection of landscapes of the local area, but selling them is proving more difficult than I'd thought, because there's such limited scope and I've not been here long enough to have made any useful connections.

Then, one morning, I bump into Lizzie in the post office. She grabs me by the arm as if I'm the answer to her prayers, which apparently I am, as moments later I've agreed to make up the numbers in her pub quiz team.

I balk at first. I'm sociable by nature, but that nature seems to have changed a little since I came here. This, I know, is connected with my need for privacy, but I can't hide away in Sunrise Cottage for the rest of the summer, and the people I've met so far have been nothing but kind.

'Yes, go on, then,' I tell Lizzie, and her face lights up.

'Seven o'clock tonight.'

'*Tonight?*'

'Yes, and don't be late. Fred likes us to start on the dot.'

When I arrive at The Rose and Crown, a solidly built 1930s white-painted pub set back off the road, there's just time for Lizzie to introduce me to her team-mates, and we're off. Fred, the publican, perches on a bar stool and reads the questions in a booming voice, leaving his red-faced wife, Doreen, to serve the customers who aren't in the quiz.

I'm enjoying myself so much that it's a surprise when I look up at the clock above the bar and see it's nearly ten. We've come fourth out of six teams, which Lizzie laughingly tells me is a lot better than usual. My other team members are a friendly bunch. There's Lizzie's husband, Sean, a handsome red-headed Irishman whom I never would have coupled with Lizzie at all, but I find that's often the way with other people's partners. The other women — Hannah and Ella — seem about my age. They both work full-time, away from the village, so it's not surprising that I haven't met them before. With a couple of glasses of wine inside me, I chat happily away to them, and before long I've gathered an invitation to a Sunday barbeque from Hannah and a free try-out session at Ella's evening tai chi class.

But the most interesting part of the evening is yet to come as, drink in hand, I get up and wander out of the main bar and towards the back door to get some air. The walls of the back room are hung with original paintings, charcoal drawings and linocuts. And, to my delight, there are prices on each piece.

Lizzie comes up behind me. 'Lovely, aren't they?'

'Are they from the village, the artists?'

'The man who does the linocuts lives in Fold, I think. Don't know about the others. Hey, why don't you show your paintings here? I bet they'd be snapped up!'

Lizzie looks at me, eyes sparkling with her idea, but I was there before her. Five minutes later, Fred, bless him, has agreed to give me wall space for my series of local landscapes. He's the fatherly type, all smiles and shoulder-pats, and I decide I like him very much. I like him even more when I order another round of drinks for my team and comment how busy it is tonight.

'And most nights,' Fred booms, in the same voice he used to ask the quiz questions. 'Don't fancy a couple of shifts, do you?'

'What, *me*?'

I nearly spill my drink. I've never worked behind a bar in my life, so why Fred thinks I look capable of it is beyond me. It can't be that hard, though, can it? Fred promises 'full training', which I suspect will be a quick lesson on how to pull a pint, and I put my reservations behind me and agree to a try-out on Saturday night.

As I walk home in the soft summer darkness, I'm pricing my landscapes in my mind, and calculating my weekly wage from the pub if I work on Tuesdays and Fridays during the week, as Fred suggested, and the occasional Saturday night if they're short. By the time I reach home, I feel almost rich.

★   ★   ★

The effects of last night's wine come crashing in as I wake the following morning. Sunlight bounces from the window onto the dressing table mirror and ricochets onto my eyeballs. I slide back beneath the purple-covered duvet with a groan, and then I remember it's Tuesday, my art class. I've booked Olivia Morton for her second session, and for some reason I feel a little nervous about it. I can't work out why; it was all fine the first time. My students had a lot of fun and enjoyed the challenge, and Olivia herself seemed relaxed to the extent of being blasé about the whole thing, as a true professional model would.

It must be Olivia's connection to Max that is making me apprehensive, I decide. I have a ridiculous image in my mind of Olivia tripping around Robin Hill, feather duster in hand, stark naked. This, I know, is a product of the turmoil that still lurks in the back of my mind, courtesy of Jayden Fox. A little of this turmoil — okay, a lot of it — also owes itself to Max himself. He tried to kiss me, and I wanted him to, so much. How I found the strength to resist him, I'll never know. But I did, and that's how it must stay.

By the time I arrive at the village hall, I feel more relaxed. My students eagerly arrange the chairs in a semicircle while I drag out the red velvet sofa and bank it with cushions to make Olivia comfortable. We're having a go at painting her today, and there's a friendly scuffle in the kitchen as water jars are fetched and filled. And then we wait, but there's no sign of our model.

'That's that, then,' announces Kevin, slapping his hands down on his knees. 'We've put her off and she's not coming back.'

Malcolm sniffs loudly. 'If anyone's put her off, it's you, talking about her nethers.'

And then everyone talks at once, all offering theories as to why we have no model today, until I hold up my hand and perform the nursery-school clap.

'*Nobody* has put Olivia off. If she wasn't coming, she'd have let me know. Why don't you do a bit of sketching while we wait?'

But my own words feel hollow as the

time drips by, and there's still no sign of our model. And then suddenly the hall door bursts open and there's Olivia, wearing faded jeans carefully ripped at the knee, and a floaty white tunic top that looks amazing on her but would seem like Gran's nightie on me.

'I'm so sorry, Violet,' she says, coming towards me. 'Maria's had a fall and sprained her ankle, so I got delayed.'

'No worries,' I say, smiling at Olivia and wondering why I'd got so het up about her. 'These things happen. I hope she's okay, your childminder?'

'Oh yes, her daughter's there taking care of her, but it means she can't have Anna.'

And with that, Olivia goes out again and moments later pushes back through the door with a small girl in a buggy. She's a mini version of her mother, all glossy dark hair, creamy complexion and big brown eyes which she fixes solemnly on me as she sums me up. And then her little face breaks out in toothy grin and

I'm smitten. Judging by the *ahs* and *oohs* going on around me, so is everyone else.

'Is it all right if she stays, just this once?' Olivia says. 'She'll be as quiet as a mouse. She'll probably drop off to sleep.'

I stoop down to stroke the toddler's hand and she gives me a dribbly smile. 'Of course she can stay. Have her close to you, by the side of the sofa.'

Well, what else can I do? It's not the best scenario, but no Anna means no Olivia, and my students are itching to get started now.

In a way, I'm thinking later, as I do the rounds and give help to those who need it, this minor disruption has broken the ice, if there was any to break. I find I'm able to forget about Olivia working for Max and see her for who she is, a single mum juggling her life to make the best of it. I do wonder, though, where Anna's father is, and if he's still on the scene. You can't judge by appearances, I know, but it seems almost a travesty, somebody as beautiful as Olivia being single.

Anna doesn't drop off to sleep, nor is she as quiet as the proverbial mouse. Instead, she yells to be liberated from the buggy five minutes into Olivia's pose, but that's to be expected, and we carry on as best we can. It's a livelier class than normal, with a two-year-old racing round the hall, sounding like a herd of baby elephants. I deliberately shorten the tea break and get everyone to finish up twenty minutes before time. Obviously relieved, Olivia hurries to get dressed and chats to me as she fastens a protesting Anna back into her buggy. Again, I think this has worked out well, as we're on friendlier terms now, and I wonder if I'll bump into Olivia again before our next session in two weeks' time.

'I live at Sunrise Cottage,' I say lightly, as Olivia bundles her dressing gown into the net thing beneath the buggy. 'It's in Clayfoot Lane, not far from Robin Hill, Max Finch's house.'

I'm giving her chance to pick up on this, and then I might invite her for a drink and a chat if she's passing. But she gives me a surprised look, which makes me think I've said something wrong.

'Yes, I know,' she says, breaking eye contact.

Does she mean she knows where Sunrise Cottage is, or that I live there? Either way, I have the distinct impression she doesn't want to be friends, which is a shame — but then, why should she? She's come here to do a job, not to make friends with me.

Malcolm comes over to check what we're doing in class next week, some of the others join us, and by the time we've finished talking, Olivia and Anna have left.

*   *   *

The sun's disappeared behind a bank of sullen cloud as I drive home, and a few spots of rain appear on the windscreen. I dismiss my plans for a *plein air* painting session this afternoon, but I don't mind. A cosy afternoon working on a couple of landscapes I've already started will be just as nice.

As always, the cottage welcomes me home, wrapping its peacefulness around me. I say 'hello' out loud to Granny Violet — I do this sometimes, daft though it is — then go through to the kitchen and see what's in the fridge for my lunch. With a satisfying, if slightly unusual, teaching session behind me and an afternoon in my studio in front of me, a glass of wine seems just the thing. I won't need to drive again today. I take a bottle from the fridge and pour some into one of Gran's crystal glasses.

Remembering there was a letter on the mat when I came in, I go back to the hallway, glass in hand. I almost spill the wine as I look down at the long white envelope.

I see you ignored my last instruction. You'll go NOW if you know what's good for you.

I look round fearfully, glancing out of the window as if there's someone watching me. But it's broad daylight, and there's nobody about, not that I can see. It's stupid to be scared of a note from an anonymous busybody, I know, but for a few minutes that is how I feel.

The note — on a torn strip of paper, same handwriting as before, with a couple of messy crossings-out — finds its way beneath the clock on the mantelpiece with the first one. Now it seems sensible to keep them, just in case. In case of *what*? I down a long slug of wine, and before long I'm able to put the whole thing into perspective. This is my house, my home, for now. I've been made welcome in the village by everyone I've met so far. To my knowledge, I've hurt nobody, upset nobody, and it seems inconceivable that there's somebody out there who resents my being here. Even more inconceivable that they'd go so far as to send threatening notes through the post.

Back in the kitchen, I top up my wine glass, then sit down at the table. My appetite seems to have waned. What were you supposed to do in these circumstances? Should I go to the nearest police station and show them the notes? Straight away I realise the pointlessness of that. Two notes, weeks apart. Not exactly bombarded with the things, am I? No mysterious phone calls, no intruders, no enemies. Nothing for the police to get a handle on. They'd drop the notes into a file and send me on my merry way.

Right. I stand up again. Whoever is playing silly games will not get the better of me. I won't be scared, and I certainly won't be hounded out of the village. I'm probably not their target, anyway, just somebody who looks like somebody else.

'Cheers!' I raise my glass in the silent kitchen, to my silent adversary. 'Waste your time with your stupid notes. I don't care!'

It works, kind of. But I'm dimly

8

Max didn't want to leave Robin Hill. True, it was a large house for one person, and for weeks at a time he would only move between his study, the bedroom and en-suite, and the kitchen — and occasionally the spacious attics where he stored some of his stock — but that didn't lessen his appreciation of the rest of the place.

Not all of his memories of Robin Hill were happy ones. Some from the Sarah days could induce a sickening swing of anxiety if he dwelt on them. But there'd been a lot of happy times, too, especially in the early days. He'd heard it said that a house could pick up on miserable times, and that sadness somehow permeated its walls and made it a less desirable place to live, but Robin Hill had no such vibe about it. It was just home.

Fair was fair, though. Legally, half the house belonged to Sarah — morally, more than half — and he would move elsewhere in a heartbeat if his ex-wife came round to the same view.

Leaving the village altogether, though, was unthinkable, now that he'd met Violet Brooke. *Sweet Violet*. He didn't regret trying to kiss her. He might not have succeeded, but at least now she knew he had feelings for her, and it wasn't as if she'd been offended. Quite the opposite. He'd sensed in the way she'd held him, and in her expression, that she'd wanted that kiss as much as he did. But what she didn't want was a relationship, because she was only staying in Fold for the summer. Or so she said. Arrogant it might be, but Max couldn't help thinking that he could be the one to change her mind about that.

Even if she did go back to London, Sunrise Cottage was hers; she'd be unlikely to abandon it completely. And as for that pillock Jayden Fox, as far as Max was concerned he was well and truly off the scene, otherwise he'd have been here by now, or Violet would have gone back to him. All this was wishful thinking, of course.

Max was still thinking about Violet when he heard the front door open. Sitting at his desk in the upstairs study with the view of the upward-sloping back garden, he'd hardly begun on the paperwork spread out in front of him but had been dreaming out of the window instead. Now he got up and went to the top of the stairs.

'Hi Max,' Olivia called up.

And then a small voice echoed her with a high-pitched, 'Hi Max!'

'Ah . . . '

'Yes, sorry. My childminder's out of action. You don't mind, do you?'

'No, of course not. There's juice and stuff in the fridge, biscuits in the cupboard. Let her have what she wants.'

'Thanks.'

Olivia held the child's hand and gazed up the wide staircase at Max, smiling gratefully. In her other hand was her usual sports bag which he knew contained the grey trackies and baggy T-shirt she changed into before she started work.

Max retreated to his study and closed the door. Olivia's daughter — Anna? — was a cute little kid. A bit noisy — at least, she had been the last time — but no trouble. It must be hard, bringing up a child on your own, and he'd never object.

Sarah was the one who'd hired Olivia to help in the house in the first place. Max had thought they could manage perfectly well on their own, but Sarah had been adamant. That was six years ago, at a time when the storms within their marriage were becoming all too frequent, and Max had easily given in because he didn't want to cause any further upset.

The way things had turned out, with Sarah getting ill, Olivia had proved to be a godsend. He had considered letting her go when he and Sarah were finally over and she moved out, but by then he'd become used to finding the bathroom and kitchen spotless, the furniture dust-free, and even his shirts ironed — although he'd never asked her to do that — and he'd let it ride.

Olivia had suffered stormy times of her own during her employment at Robin Hill. When she'd fallen pregnant, Max hadn't noticed anything amiss, which Sarah had said was typical of a man; but of course, as time went on, it had become obvious even to him. According to Sarah, Olivia's relationship with whoever the father was had not been straightforward, and she'd split up from him while the baby was only a few months old. But Olivia, understandably, had been tight-lipped about her personal life, and even Sarah hadn't been privy to all the details, although Max suspected she'd have preferred it otherwise. When Olivia went off to have her baby, he'd thought that was the last they'd seen of her, but four months later, she was back at Robin Hill to resume her duties as if nothing had happened.

His mind hijacked first by Violet and now by Olivia, Max gave up on his paperwork and went downstairs.

'Coffee or tea?' Olivia said, smiling as he entered the kitchen.

'You read my mind. Coffee, please. Instant will do.'

'Nope. Machine's on.'

'Lovely. Thanks.'

It was kind of her to make him proper coffee when she didn't drink it herself, he thought. Sometimes he wondered how she managed to anticipate his needs so accurately.

He went and stood against the granite-topped island, watching Olivia moving purposefully around his kitchen with a sense of ownership, which was enhanced by the sight of the child whom he could see through the window roly-polying down the grass bank.

His mind veered off at a wild angle as he imagined what it would be like if this *was* Olivia's kitchen: her house, in fact. According to Sarah, at the height of one of her manic episodes, that was exactly what he wanted: Olivia Morton in both his kitchen and his bed. She'd even accused him of having already slept with her. As if that wasn't bad enough, she'd then gone and accused Olivia to her face of seducing her husband.

It had been a mortifying experience all round. But Olivia wasn't stupid. She'd known exactly how the land lay regarding Sarah, but she'd kept a low profile for a while, avoiding Max as much as she could, even after Sarah had made a dramatic and tearful apology. Max couldn't blame her. He felt the same.

'The postman came, by the way,' Olivia said, passing Max his mug of coffee.

'Right, I'll go and . . . '

'I picked it up and put it over there, on the side.'

Max took his post and coffee upstairs. His phone rang as soon as he'd sat down at his desk, a call from a fellow dealer tipping him off about some art deco items in a forthcoming sale. They talked for a while, and then Max remembered a couple of calls he'd meant to make himself. Returning finally to the paperwork, he dealt with the urgent stuff, then fired up the laptop to check his emails and carry out a bit of research.

It was a while before he got around to opening his post. There were four items. An invoice for sellers' fees from his regular auction house, something about road widening from the council, a credit card statement, and . . . what was this? Max frowned at the strip of paper with a biro scrawl across it:

Stay away from Sunrise Cottage or you'll be sorry.

Blimey. Max stared at the message. He couldn't take it in. Who would make a threat like that, and *why?* Dropping the piece of paper onto the desk, he steepled his hands against his mouth. As far as he was aware, nobody knew of his relationship with Violet, such as it was — this had to be about Violet. Had somebody seen him going into her cottage,? And even if they had, what was it to them?

He examined the envelope. It had his name and address, with postcode and everything, printed on a stuck-on label, and a first class stamp, giving no clue as to its origins. The writing on the message was scruffy. One of the 't's in *Cottage* had originally been missed out and squeezed in afterwards.

There was a tap on the door, and before he could say anything, it opened and Olivia put her head round. Max shoved the offending missive beneath the other post, but she didn't come any further into the room. He saw her glance at the desk before she gave him a bright smile.

'Shall I hang the washing out before I go? It's nearly finished.'

Max looked at the time. Olivia had completed her hours for today, and the little girl was now by her side, jigging up and down, pulling on her mother's sleeve. Besides, and more to the point, the wash he'd put on earlier contained mostly his boxers and bed-shorts.

'No, no, you get off now. I'll stick it all in the tumble dryer.'

'Well, if you're sure. It's no trouble. If there's anything extra you need doing any time, you only have to say.'

'Yes, I know. And thanks, Olivia.'

Max was puzzled. He didn't usually have this kind of conversation with Olivia. She arrived, she did her stuff in the order she decided was best, and left. Sometimes there was small talk as their paths crossed. Otherwise, there wasn't a lot of contact.

He heard Olivia's car pull away. A heavy silence descended over the house. He thought about walking along to Violet's to see if she was all right, but he had no real reason to go there; and he couldn't tell her about the note, not without frightening her half to death. He'd planned to open the shop for the afternoon. Little Barton was one of the prettiest villages in the area, and attracted a steady flow of tourists. In summer he stood a couple of tables outside with a selection of the cheaper stuff. Mostly, people just browsed and moved on, but a few would buy. It was boring, being in the shop. Really he only kept it as a storage place and shop window, but the way he felt now, with his head all over the place, boring would be just the ticket.

He drove the long way round so that he could pass Sunrise Cottage, but there was no sign of Violet, no sighting which would give him an excuse to stop and say hello.

Arriving at the shop, he almost turned round and went home again. The window looked decidedly dusty and depressing — his fault for not shifting the stock around often enough — but he was here now, so he may as well stay for an hour or so. Before opening up, he nipped across the road to the bakery and bought a pasty and a cold drink for his lunch. Deciding he couldn't be bothered to put the tables out today, he propped the door wide so that anyone could see he was open, then sat down in the old chair he kept behind the counter.

The note was in his pocket. He'd put it there so there was no likelihood of Olivia finding it, should she happen to dust next time she came. In truth, he'd rather she didn't touch his desk as she did tend to tidy it too much, but she did it with all good intentions and he didn't have the heart to tell her not to.

He stared at the writing, not knowing what to make of it. Nothing like this had happened to him before. What were you supposed to do? Dismiss it as a prank, or as the work of some poor soul who'd flipped their lid? Inform the police? What?

And then it came to him: Jayden Fox, Violet's ex-boyfriend. From what Max had read in the papers, the man was a bit off-beam, a bit wacky. Had he come to Sussex after all and been scouting about, seeing what he could find? Had he, in fact, come to see Violet?

Max slapped himself on the forehead. He had no idea whether Violet had been seeing Jayden, broken engagement or not. That part, the part where she'd fled London and had nothing more to do with him, Max had made up to suit his own purposes, when actually he had no idea. Violet had kept her background a secret from him, so how would he know what was really going on there? Suppose Fox had been trying to win Violet back, and she'd refused him, so he'd resorted to desperate measures such as writing anonymous notes . . .

. . . well, if that was the case, the guy must have done one heck of a lot of poking about to have associated him with Violet. They'd hardly spent a lot of time in one another's company, had they? He could count on one hand the number of times he'd actually been to Sunrise Cottage, more was the pity.

No, of course it wasn't Jayden Fox. He was clutching at straws; the idea was too far-fetched.

So, if not him, then who? Somebody

from the village, then, somebody with a grudge against him or against Violet. Again, this seemed ridiculous. He might not be deeply involved in village life — he preferred it that way, especially after all that stupid knocker-boy gossip that had flown around — but he was on affable terms with those he did associate with. It seemed impossible that he'd upset somebody without knowing about it. And as for Violet, everybody liked her. How could they not? She'd slipped seamlessly into village life and he could tell from the things she said that she was already popular.

As if on cue, Max's mobile trembled in his pocket. He frowned into the dim light of the shop as the name came up. Edward, his father-in-law. Well, ex-father-in-law.

'Max? Edward.'

'Yes, hi, how are you?'

'Fine, we're both fine. Look, I thought I should let you know that Sarah's home, at her flat in Worthing. It's not your responsibility, of course, but you do still see her, and so we thought we should let you know, that's all.'

There was a small silence, and Max thought Edward was about to cut off the call. Sarah's parents were lovely, understanding people who had never sought to blame him in any way for the breakdown of the marriage, no more than they had blamed their daughter. Actually, he rather missed seeing them, especially as he had no living parents of his own. It was sad that their only contact now was directly related to Sarah's illness.

'Yes, thank you for letting me know. It's kind of you, Edward, and I'm really glad she's better. Give her my love, won't you, and tell her I'll see her soon?'

'Yes, yes . . . ' Edward sounded flustered, a bit uncertain. 'Max, I wasn't going to mention this, but it's best that you're fully in the picture. Sarah wasn't sent home because she was completely well again. She discharged herself, yesterday afternoon.'

* * *

Max looked at the note again, closely. *Sarah?* It didn't look much like her handwriting, but it was scribbled, and he hadn't seen an example of her writing for ages. Besides, who knew what tricks her poor mind was playing on her? Sarah's illness had already changed her in ways he'd never have thought possible. But how would she know about Violet, and Sunrise Cottage?

He thought for a minute. Like him, Sarah had never fully involved herself in village life, apart from the sewing bee which she'd run for a while — sewing was Sarah's special skill. Embroidery, tapestry, that sort of thing. She'd taught it professionally, at a higher education college. One of the women in the village had been an especially keen member of the sewing bee, and she and Sarah had been friends. In fact — Max stared unseeingly out of the window, thinking hard — yes, the woman, whose name he'd forgotten, had once asked him how Sarah was when he'd bumped into her in the chemist. They'd kept in touch, apparently, which had surprised Max, but he'd thought no more of it at the time.

That was some while ago now; but suppose the contact had been kept up, and this woman had been feeding Sarah tales about him — and, more worryingly, about Violet? If it was Sarah who'd sent the note, she definitely wasn't well, and he should do something about it. But his hands were tied there. Edward was right: she was no longer his responsibility. All he could do for now was keep a surreptitious eye on Violet and hope that nothing else happened.

Max smiled to himself, the first time he'd felt like smiling since he'd read that ridiculous poison-pen note. Stay away? Like that was ever going to happen. He couldn't wait to see Violet again.

9

Sarah was still in her dressing gown when she opened the door to her sister, Polly.

'Hey, what's this? Late night, was it?' Polly came into the hall and gave Sarah a hug. 'No, don't tell me. I don't need the sordid details.'

Sarah laughed. Her sister knew very well there were no details, sordid or otherwise. Nor a late night either, not of the kind she meant. Bless Polly! She'd never fussed and flapped around her, not even at the height of her illness, when she was at her craziest one moment and mired in deepest depression the next.

'Seriously, Sis, are you really okay? It wasn't just a spur of the moment thing, walking out of Maytree Grange?'

'No, it wasn't *spur of the moment*. I thought about it and decided it was

148

time I took control, that's all. Besides, I'm much better off here than sitting around all day, being waited on hand and foot.'

Polly sniffed. 'Yes, well, I wouldn't mind some of that.'

Polly worked four days a week as a receptionist in a chiropodists' practice. The rest of her time was taken up with running around after four grown men, as she put it; the four men in question being Polly's husband and three teenage sons.

'Is it your day off?' Sarah automatically slippered her way to the kitchen and flicked the kettle on.

'It's Sunday . . . Sarah, are you sure you're okay?'

'Sunday, of course. I knew that.'

'I escaped,' Polly said, sitting down at the kitchen table. 'Miles is playing golf and the boys are off doing whatever it is they do. I thought you and I could go out for coffee.'

'Out?'

'Yes, out. You know. Beyond these

walls. Sky and stuff.'

Sarah gathered herself. She felt as if she was wading through treacle this morning. It was those damn tablets. But she'd practically sworn an oath that she'd take them properly, otherwise they would never have let her leave the premises, let alone get a taxi to the station and the train to Worthing on her own.

'Where are the girls?' Polly looked around the kitchen, and out of the window at Sarah's pretty walled garden.

'Through there, fast asleep. I do miss them, when I'm away, and I'm sure they miss me too.'

She went through the arch to the living room, Polly following. Bronte and Hermione, grey Persian cats with amazing amber eyes, were curled up on the mustard-yellow sofa amongst the vibrant banks of embroidered cushions. Two fur heaps rose and fell gently. Bronte twitched an ear.

'They were perfectly fine while you were away,' Polly said, perching on the arm of the sofa and gently stroking the hump of Hermione's back. 'I came by several times, and Mum and Dad popped over. Your friends upstairs did a great job of feeding them.'

'I know. I'm very lucky.' Sarah looked around her cosy room with its jade and turquoise curtains, creamy walls, and framed examples of her embroidery and tapestry. She gave a little satisfied sigh. 'Oh, I have missed all this. My little flat, my lovely home.'

Tears glazed her eyes. Polly saw, and put on her no-nonsense voice.

'Now then, none of that. Get showered and dressed. I need that coffee and some sea air.'

* * *

'Have you heard anything from Max lately?' Polly asked, after they'd left a café and were strolling along the sea-front towards Worthing pier.

She'd always championed Max. Sarah had always suspected she fancied him, although she'd never admit it.

'I have seen him, as it happens. He came to the Grange.' Sarah slowed her step, casting her mind back. 'I think I might not have talked very much. I was so tired.'

'He won't have minded.'

'Won't he?' Sarah gave a kind of snort. 'How would I know what Max minds and what he doesn't?'

That wasn't fair. Polly didn't need this, not when she was being so kind. Everybody was so kind, including Max. Sarah wasn't sure she deserved it.

'He's been a star, Max has,' she admitted.

'Yep, a right little shiner. Shall we sit here for a bit?' Polly was already heading for a bench set between raised flower beds.

'Max keeps saying we should sell Robin Hill,' Sarah said, after they'd sat for a while, gazing out at the milky blue horizon. 'He's got an ulterior motive, of course.'

'Surely he's saying that for your sake,

because it's the right thing to do? You own half that house. If I were you, I wouldn't chuck it back in his face.'

'He says it's for me, but d'you know what I think? I think it's his way of saying a final goodbye. A way to get shot of me for good. That's why he's pressing me to sell up our family home.'

'Sarah, is he *really* pressing you? That doesn't sound a bit like Max to me. Anyway, haven't all the goodbyes been said, more than once, especially when the decree came through? Goodbyes don't come much more final than that.'

'He told me he wants to move on, to a new woman. One who isn't half-mad like me.' She gave a little laugh.

Polly didn't reply. She looked doubtfully at Sarah and shook her head slowly.

'Okay, I might have got that a bit mixed up. But in essence, that's what he meant.'

'He is entitled, Sarah. You haven't been a couple for years. You can't begrudge him a new love and a bit of happiness, surely?'

'I don't begrudge him. If you must know, I told him to go out and find somebody else.'

She had said that, she remembered now. What she couldn't remember was whether she'd meant it. Whether she'd really felt it, inside. Sometimes words came out of her mouth of their own accord. Sometimes a lot of things happened of their own accord, and then she was left wondering what on earth she'd done, and why.

'Yes, well,' Polly said, then backtracked to the subject of Robin Hill, clearly thinking Max's love life was an unsafe topic. 'Why doesn't he buy you out of the house, give you the money for your half? That would solve the problem.'

'There isn't a problem, not unless Max makes it into one. Anyway, he can't afford to buy me out. You've seen the house, it's in a desirable area. Not that I desire it, not in any shape or form.'

She'd never wanted to live in the country. That had been Max's idea, which she'd gone along with because she loved him. She'd much rather live somewhere with a bit of life. When she'd finally made the break, she'd considered moving to Brighton, but her sister was in Worthing, their parents just outside it. For once in her life she'd made a good decision and found her gorgeous garden flat in a converted Edwardian house, five minutes' walk from the sea.

'I never thought it was quite you, living out in the sticks,' Polly said dreamily. 'The things we do for love.'

Neither of them spoke for a while. Polly rested her head on the back of the bench and closed her eyes. Sarah gazed at her brown feet in sandals, poking out from the hem of her long skirt, one she'd run up herself from a length of floral cotton she'd found in the market. So much more satisfying than buying new from a high-street shop. You could never get the kind of thing you wanted there, anyway.

She thought back to her working days

at the college, where she'd taught her students about needlework and textiles and design. They were good days, at the beginning. The practical side was lovely, but she'd found the administrative side taxing, because of her dyslexia. She hadn't even been able to fill in the mark sheets without constant crossings-out and making an embarrassing holy mess of the whole thing.

The department had closed eventually, the courses merged with another college. By that time, she'd had enough anyway. She'd just begun to look for another job when the stupid illness descended and sent her mind flying every which way.

Polly's phone cut through Sarah's musings with its trilly tune.

'I've got to go,' she said, sitting up and looking at the screen. 'The boys are back. They'll want lunch.'

'Can't they get their own?'

'You wouldn't say that if you saw the mess they make. Come on, I'll walk back with you first.'

10

I've decided I like working at The Rose and Crown, now that I've got the hang of the pumps, the optics, the till, and the other million things there are to know about. This is my fourth shift, my second Friday night, and Max has been in since nine-thirty. He's sitting across from the bar, chatting to a middle-aged couple I don't recognise. Earlier, he was sitting with Kevin from my art group, and his wife. Despite Max telling me he doesn't get involved in village life, he seems to know quite a few people, enough to have plenty to talk about.

Doreen served him when he first came in, but he had a chat with me while he waited for his pint. It felt like small talk, the way he might converse with any other bartender, and I couldn't help feeling disappointed.

Well, what did I expect? He tried to

157

kiss me and I rejected him. I don't know whether to be pleased or sorry that he's backed off. I'm not usually so confused, but where Max is concerned, that's precisely how I am.

There's a sudden rush as a group of young men arrive, and it's not until I serve the last pint and look up that I see Max standing at the bar. He's wearing dark blue jeans, to just the right degree of tightness, and a white shirt with the top three buttons undone. He smiles, and my heart flips.

'Have a drink with me?'

I return the smile. 'Okay. Thanks.'

I have a vodka tonic, my second of the night. It's a large one, because Max insists and Fred, overhearing, jovially backs him up. Max has a whisky chaser.

Once our drinks are on the bar, I don't know what to say. It's as if my store of chat for the night has dried up. Or perhaps it's because I'm only the bar's width away from Max Finch.

'You look great, by the way,' he says.

I've left my hair loose and I'm

wearing a black off-the-shoulder top, something I used to use in London to glam up a pair of jeans, as it does now. I've made up my eyes a little, too, and put on lip-gloss.

'Thanks.' I smile at Max. 'You look good, too. Love the shirt.' It's the drink talking, but I don't care.

Max looks surprised. 'It's just a white shirt, but thanks.'

I lean a little way towards him, across the bar. 'There isn't a bloke on earth who doesn't look good in a white shirt.'

This is absolutely true. Jayden agreed with me. He had six of them.

'Is that so?' Max's eyes twinkle. 'I shall have to wear it more often then, shan't I?'

'You should,' I say, twinkling back.

Oh God, I've done it now. What's he supposed to make of me flirting with him after turning him down flat? Talk about mixed messages. Hopefully he knows it's vodka-induced.

He mentions my three watercolour landscapes which are now hanging in the back room, complete with modest — but not too modest — price-tags, and then our chat is interrupted by the last-orders customers. Max stays where he is throughout, and when I've served the last person, he asks if he can walk me home. Since he has to pass my door to reach his own, I can hardly refuse. Then I remember I cycled here.

The bike is not a problem, apparently. Max insists on wheeling it for me, and half-way along the high street he mounts up and wobbles off along the pavement, making wild hand signals, while I collapse into giggles at the sight of him on a ladies' bike with a basket on the front.

We seem to take an age to reach Sunrise Cottage; unsurprising, as we've been messing about with the bike most of the way. Max wheels it up the garden path for me and props it against the side wall, where I tell him I keep it. There's the tiniest awkward moment while I stand at the front door, keys in hand, and Max stands on the path, making no attempt to leave.

'Violet . . . '

'Max . . . '

Our voices collide. Neither of us says any more. I have no idea what I was going to say anyway, except it feels like I should say something. Then Max places his hands on my waist and pulls me to him, and this time encounters no resistance from me as he claims a kiss.

★   ★   ★

The Saturday art club at the comprehensive school has finished for the summer, but I can manage without it, now I have my bar work. It's good to be free on a Saturday, and this morning I take my time over my bath and breakfast.

My mind, naturally, is on Max and what happened last night. I didn't ask him in, although I felt I could have done without giving him expectations I'm nowhere near ready to fulfil. But we talked a little, between kisses, and he

161

agreed that we should take things slowly, enjoy each other's company, and not worry about the future. I reminded Max again that come summer's end, I'll be gone. He made a sad face, but it was a kind of jokey one.

Neither of us wants to be the source of village gossip, however innocuous it may be, and for now we're keeping our relationship a secret — as far as anything can be kept secret in Fold. I was also thinking about those threatening notes, although for some reason I didn't want to tell Max about them. The idea of there being somebody out there who wants rid of me sounds too far-fetched to be genuine, but I'd rather not give them reason to hike up their little campaign by being seen around with Max.

I switch the radio on while I wash up my breakfast things and tidy round. On the floor beside the inglenook is a pile of art magazines. As I flick through to check which ones I've finished with, I come across three auction catalogues:

the two I sent away for, and one I picked up from the place I went to with Max. My Chelsea tea-service isn't listed in any of them, and I can't think now why I was so bothered in the first place.

I put the catalogues in the recycling box with the art magazines and close the lid firmly. At the same time, I close the lid on my doubts about Max's honesty concerning my china. Remembering his arms round me last night, his kisses that were even more gorgeous than I'd imagined, I feel guilty for thinking badly of him, and thankful he has no idea.

★   ★   ★

Later, I ride down to the village, and I'm coming out of the little supermarket in Fold's high street when I see Olivia Morton drive by. Then, as I'm thinking about treating myself to a coffee in Cherry on the Top, I notice her car has stopped and she's backing up, as if it's an afterthought. When she's almost level with me, she winds the passenger window down and leans across.

'Hi.' I duck down to her level. Anna, in her car seat in the back, beams at me and I smile back.

'Hi,' Olivia says. 'I see you've got shopping. Can I give you a lift home?'

'Oh, that's kind, but I cycled down. My bike's chained up along there.' I nod along the street.

'But you've got bags.'

'Only a couple. They'll go on the handlebars. I'm used to it. I tell you what, though, I was just going to grab a coffee. Why don't you and Anna come too?'

Olivia seems to jump at this, as if I've suggested a marvellous treat, and then I think that with looking after Anna she probably doesn't have much chance to sit around in cafés.

Cherry on the Top is really busy, as it always is on a Saturday morning, but we find ourselves a tiny table in a corner. Suddenly I feel a little awkward. I hardly know Olivia, but I suppose this is my chance to get to know her better. At the same time I'm acutely aware of the link between us: Max. It's a weird situation, with me knowing about that and Olivia not. I wonder if she'll mention him, and if so, will I be able to keep my face neutral? Perhaps this wasn't such a good idea.

I order a latte with a rosette of cream on top. Olivia orders a lemon and ginger tea. When we have our drinks, we chat about the village and the area in general, and it's pretty easygoing. Little Anna behaves beautifully, chatting and smiling away in between noisy sucks on her juice straw and nibbles of her strawberry-and-white-chocolate cupcake. I remark on this to Olivia, and her response knocks me sideways.

'Yes, she's a good little thing. I wouldn't be without her. Unlike others. Anna's biological father left her, left *us*, before she was three months old. I call him her biological father because that's all he ever was. All he ever will be.'

I don't know what I'm meant to say

to this. Olivia has elevated me from casual acquaintance to confidante in one leap.

'It must have been difficult for you, bringing Anna up on your own.' Realising this might not be accurate, I add, 'If you have been on your own, the whole time . . . ? Sorry, I shouldn't have said that. Forget it.'

'No, it's fine. I've had a couple of relationships since. If you can call them that. But they didn't work out. Oh *God*, do they *ever*?' She flounces her shoulders in a melodramatic gesture.

She looks pointedly at me, as if she's hoping for similar intimate details. If so. I'm sorry to disappoint her.

I smile ruefully. 'I've not had a lot of luck in that direction myself.'

Olivia gives an understanding nod, then Anna provides a welcome distraction by holding out her icing-sticky hands, and Olivia dives into her bag for a wet-wipe.

She asks me how long I'm renting Sunrise Cottage for. Okay, it's a left-field question, but she's just being friendly. I tell her a little about Granny Violet and how the cottage came into my possession.

'It's the perfect summer retreat,' I say. 'I'm very lucky.'

'Ooh, I *do* envy you,' Olivia says, with a smile that tells me she's not serious. 'It's such a sweet little cottage. I go past it three times a week. Anna and I live in a cottage, too, though it's not as pretty as yours. It's an old quarry-worker's cottage, in a terrace of six. We're on the Little Barton Road.'

'It sounds lovely.'

'It does us. It's rented, of course. I don't own it, not like you do yours.'

And now I am detecting the merest smidgeon of real envy in Olivia's tone.

'Yes, well, as I say, I got lucky. I couldn't afford a property in this part of the world otherwise.'

'Not if you're on your own.'

'No.'

I finish my coffee and change the subject.

'My art students are pleased you're

modelling for them. They need challenging.'

'My body's a challenge, is it?'

Olivia laughs, and so do I. My faux pas has brought normality back, and I'm relieved.

'You know what I mean. All life drawing is challenging, especially if you're new to it.'

We're both laughing now, and I decide I like Olivia. Her directness is refreshing.

She tells me about other places where she's modelled, and in some cases still does, apparently. I listen with interest, and then I make another faux pas, only this time Olivia has no idea.

'I'm sorry the modelling doesn't pay more,' I say. 'The council won't fork out a penny over the standard rate, and that's pathetic enough as it is. Well, of course you know that.'

Olivia gives a knowing nod. 'Good thing I don't rely on it. I have my job at Robin Hill, down the road from you. I take care of the domestic side, mainly.

Max Finch is an antique dealer, top end. You might know him?'

Olivia's face seems closer to mine than before. But it's a very small table, so . . .

'I know Robin Hill,' I say, neatly skirting the question as I regret raising the subject of pay and employment. 'It's a beautiful house. I admire it every time I go past.'

'It is. I love working there. Actually, I'm more of a personal assistant to Max than a housekeeper.'

Personal assistant?

'That's nice.'

It's an inane reply, but the best I can do. I hate being dishonest, but if I admit I know Max, Olivia won't leave it at that, and I'll be pitched into keeping up a charade.

I look at my watch, rather desperately.

'Is that the time? I must go,' I say, standing up. 'You and Anna must pop into mine for a cup of tea.' Then, remembering Olivia doesn't drink ordinary tea, I add vaguely, 'Or something.'

Why did I say that? Anna, bless her, chooses that moment to demand to be taken to the toilet and I make my escape, wondering if Olivia will turn up at Sunrise Cottage; and, if she does, how I'm going to keep up the pretence about Max. Keeping my personal life private, and Max's too, isn't going to be easy, but I'm determined to try.

★   ★   ★

Max and I are sitting — well, lying, to be precise — on top of Fold Hill one afternoon when he tells me something that surprises me, although there's no reason why it should.

'Violet, I know there's nothing heavy going on with us, but I think I should tell you about Sarah.'

'Sarah?'

For a funny moment there, I thought he was going to say 'Olivia' — she's been on my mind a bit since our get-together.

'Yes. Sarah's my ex-wife, only she

170

hasn't been ex for very long. To cut a long story short, our marriage was over, in effect, years ago, but she got sick and we didn't get around to divorcing until recently. In February this year.'

He props his head up on his elbow and looks at me to see how I'm taking this news. I knew Max must have history, of course, but somehow I'd gained the impression he'd been single for a long time.

February. Around the time I ran away from Jayden and my life in London, Max was changing his life too. I feel the connection like an invisible thread running between us. My emotions seem close to the surface today, and I'm filled with sadness for both of us.

'Hey, hey. What's all this?'

Max wipes away a single tear from my cheekbone with his thumb, and it's such a tender, intimate gesture that it makes me want to cry properly. But this isn't about me. It's about Max, and clearly he wants to tell me more. I sit up and clasp my hands round my knees.

'What sort of sick?'

'Cyclothymia. It's a mild form of bipolar disorder. Her symptoms aren't an exact fit, but that's the closest diagnosis they could get.'

'Oh Max, I'm so sorry. How awful for her. And you, of course.'

'Yup, it's grim, but she has her good days — a lot of good days, thankfully — and the medication keeps her on an even keel. The problem is she sometimes stops taking the tablets, and then the whole thing becomes wildly unpredictable. There's nothing more to say, really. I just thought you should be fully in the picture because I do still have contact with Sarah.'

Max goes on to tell me that Sarah has a flat in Worthing, and that when she needs treatment or rest, she goes into residential care somewhere near Petersfield. I want to ask how often he sees her, but I don't want him to get the wrong idea. I'm genuinely interested, but not because I'm jealous or anything like that. He tells me anyway.

'I see her every couple of months, no more. Mine and Sarah's finances are still entwined in some respects, and I still care about her. Not in a romantic way, but our divorce was by mutual agreement — probably the most amicable it could get — and I don't want to cut away from her completely. I will in time, but not yet.'

'Of course. I understand. I'm so sorry, Max. I don't know what else to say, nothing that would help.'

Max sits up and puts his arm around my shoulders. I lean into him, and then he kisses me.

'I don't need you to say anything,' he says, when we break away. 'But I think it's only fair that you know who I am, and about what's important in my life, before . . . well, in case we get more deeply involved.'

'Oh, Max . . . '

'I know. You're only here for the summer.' He smiles. 'It's okay, I get it.'

I gaze at the view for a few moments, thinking about what Max has told me. He's not yet forty, and he's already been through divorce and had to deal with the trauma of his wife's mental illness. It makes my problems with Jayden seem self-centred and insignificant, and I have a new admiration for him. Although my story doesn't match his in its intensity, it's only fair that I should open up to Max the way he has to me.

And so I begin my tale, which doesn't take very long to tell, and Max listens quietly and nods occasionally.

'Does Jayden know where you are?' he asks, when I've finished.

'Put it this way: I haven't told him, and I know my parents wouldn't either. Not that he's called them as yet, which just goes to show how little I mean to him if he hasn't even bothered to try and track me down.'

Not so long ago, thinking about that would have made me angry and sad. But I really think I'm over Jayden now, and that's progress.

'When I go back to London, it'll be to somewhere — anywhere — other than Brick Lane. I've got friends in Camden. They'll put me up, if they remember who I am.' I give a little laugh, thinking I must get in touch with some of my old mates soon. 'I can get work, the same kind of work I was doing before, teaching art in the community and in colleges, helping with social projects. There'll be opportunities in other boroughs. I'll make my way somehow, and it'll all come out right.'

Max nods, and then he slaps his hands down on his thighs. 'Jayden Fox must be a *total* idiot. I hope he knows what he's lost, and he's regretting it night and day.'

I'm about to agree when I'm brought up short. Max said 'Jayden Fox', and I'm certain I didn't mention his surname. Possibly he knew the name before and it's come back to him now, but Max isn't a follower of the modern art scene, so it's unlikely.

I look closely at Max. His expression tells me everything.

'You already knew, didn't you? You knew all the time where I came from and who I was with. I didn't need to tell you at all.'

I make a little snorting sound and turn my head away from Max. I can't believe this. Am I not entitled to any privacy?

'Violet, I'm so sorry. Please don't be upset. I would never have found out if . . . '

I turn back to face him. 'If *what*?'

Max sighs. 'If I hadn't fallen for you, right there, in the middle of that damn field. I'm sorry, Violet, but I'm only flesh and blood. You can't blame me for wanting to know every little thing about you?'

He turns his statement into a question. A question I can't find the answer to.

There are two things going on here. Firstly, Max has virtually admitted that for him it was love at first sight, which is scary enough. Secondly, he's invaded my privacy by looking me up on the internet, where presumably he found the tosh they printed about Jayden and me in the tabloids just to fill a few columns. He's known all along and said nothing. That's what galls me the most: not the fact that he knows, but that he kept his knowledge secret from me.

I'm so angry now that I can't speak. I scramble to my feet and look around, kind of wildly. All I see are a few dog-walkers and the yellow roof of Max's car, far below the brow of Fold Hill. I need to be home, tucked away, safe from the world, in Sunrise Cottage, and I need to be there now.

'Violet . . . ' Max is on his feet.

'Will you take me home, please?'

He places a hand on my arm, and looks hurt when I shake him off.

'I should have said something the minute I found out, but we weren't seeing each other at the time; and it's not as if I've discovered anything terrible about you, is it? Jayden was never charged with forgery in the end, and you weren't implicated in any way, so . . .'

'I know, and it's not that. Not really.' My shoulders relax and I manage to look Max in the eye. At least he hasn't mentioned Angelica. If he has seen the pictures of her draped around my fiancé in some nightclub, he's sensitive enough not to say so.

'When I ran out on my life that day in February, I'd reached breaking point. Jayden had stopped loving me for the simple reason he had no love left for anyone but himself. He's a brilliant artist with an immense talent, and I was so proud of him. But I'd become an extra in his life, often with the smallest walk-on part. Those paparazzi did me a favour. They saw me as the means to an end, that was all, and I knew then that it was up to me to change things, whatever sacrifices it took. Max, I came to Sunrise Cottage as a woman with her own life, her own talent and ambitions, and the means to fulfil them — alone. I've done nothing to be ashamed of — well, you know that — but that isn't the point. I wanted to shake off the past, not have it follow me around. I thought I could trust you, but apparently I was wrong.'

I take a long, shuddery breath. That was quite a speech and I feel a bit shaky. Max looks suitably impressed, but he's also contrite.

'You *can* trust me, Violet. I know it was wrong of me to probe into your background, but believe me, I'd never tell a word of that to anyone. The village can be a hotbed of tittle-tattle at times, but I don't take part in it. Anyway, you've told me yourself now.'

'So it doesn't matter any more?'

'No, I'm not saying that.' Max holds up his hands. 'Violet, I don't know what I can say to make this right, other than to say again that I'm really sorry, and I won't mention Jayden Fox again, to you or anyone else. Can you forgive me?'

My eyes sweep the wide blue sky, the

patchwork of fields below, the homely mounds of the hills beyond. And then I meet Max's appealing gaze and my stupid heart reaches out to him.

'Okay, but . . . '

Max closes the space between us in one stride and silences me with a long, tender kiss.

11

June drifts into July. The colours in the garden come from a palette of faded pastels punctuated by the fiery red of the poppies. The small lawn at the back is strewn with crinkled rose petals, and the lavender is alive with bees. I'm aware of every tiny change as the heart of Sunrise Cottage beats to the rhythm of nature. It will be hard to leave all this behind.

Leaving Max will be harder still. Sometimes, when we're together, his expression becomes distant and wistful, and I know what he's thinking. But by mutual agreement we don't talk about my returning to London, nor what will happen afterwards.

We have fun together, Max and I. He has a wry sense of humour and I'm laughing constantly. We have our favourite places: a pretty riverside pub with a great menu, theatres and cinemas in the nearby towns; and when we're free to see each other in the daytime, we head up to Fold Hill or wander the public footpaths around Fold and Little Barton. So far we've avoided visiting each other's houses, which would be sure to draw somebody's attention, even in a quiet road such as ours. I am dying to see inside Robin Hill, though, and I will soon.

So far we haven't bumped into anyone we know while we've been together, but Max perversely insists on meeting me from some of my shifts at The Rose and Crown and walking me home, oblivious to who might be watching. My bar sessions are livened by wondering if Max will walk in through the door; and when he does, we make furtive eye contact across the bar while we make tongue-in-cheek small talk.

It has its compensations, keeping our relationship secret. It's romantic and exciting. How much longer we can keep it hidden is anyone's guess, but for now it's a game we like to play.

My Tuesday art sessions are going well. Last week we had three new members: a couple of middle-aged women — Sheila and Penny — whom I already knew by sight, and a guy about my age, Jonas, who has a ponytail and chews gum constantly, to Malcolm's annoyance. Jonas has a natural talent. He's fantastic at drawing with pen, and is the envy of the group when he captures Olivia's lissom form on paper with apparently effortless ease.

Now that Olivia and I are, apparently, buddies, she takes her time dressing at the end of her sessions, chatting to me from behind the screen. Last time, I broke it to her that I only need her once every four weeks now instead of every fortnight. I want to widen our syllabus, and I've planned sessions on architecture, animals and Chinese brush painting.

There was a small silence when I gave her the news, and I guessed she was thinking of the money she'll miss, but then she popped out from behind the screen, all smiles, and told me it was fine. She also added that she might give Max an extra couple of hours. I experienced a stab of something like jealousy, which is not like me, and I wondered if it was a sign that Max and I are becoming too close.

For today's class I've persuaded everyone to join me in a *plein air* session. Luckily it's sunny, although the temperature's dropped and there's a sharp little wind which creeps up on us and whisks up the corners of our paper.

We're in the churchyard of Saint Peter's. Situated in the centre of Fold, it's easy for everyone to get to, and alongside the typically English church-yard with its ancient lichen-covered gravestones runs a row of picturesque cottages, the oldest in the village. Most of my students have chosen the cottages as their subject, while Malcolm and Marigold concentrate on the solid archi-tecture of the square-towered church itself.

It's a happy, successful morning, and nobody seems in a hurry to leave. I'm not in a hurry either, and I wait until everyone's gone before I check around to see that we haven't left any litter or possessions behind before I load my own stuff onto my bike which is leaning by the lych-gate. In the longish grass where we set up I find an eraser, a green watercolour pencil, and a half-empty packet of chewing gum which can only belong to Jonas. I wonder if he can last without it until he gets home. I add my finds to my rucksack and set off.

As I ride down my road and pass Folding Farm, the 'Eggs for Sale' sign catches my eye, and I stop off to choose a dozen large brown beauties from the sales table at the gate, dropping my money into the honesty box. I wedge the egg-box sideways into my bicycle basket because there's nowhere else for it to go. Most of the box sticks out, but it'll be fine until I get home.

I'm within sight of Sunrise Cottage's

chimney when my mind wanders and I ride straight over a stone that's more like a boulder. The bike goes one way and I go the other. I don't know what I've hit until I'm sprawled on the ground, half of me on the road and the other half on the grass verge, the contents of the bicycle basket strewn all around. I drag myself fully onto the verge and sit there while I get my breath back, cursing myself for not looking where I was going.

A car stops close by, and then there's Olivia coming towards me with a concerned expression on her face.

'Here.' She offers me an elegant hand, and I haul myself inelegantly to a vaguely upright position, which isn't easy with a heavy rucksack on my back.

'Have you done any damage?' Olivia says, frowning as she looks me up and down.

'Yes. A dozen eggs' worth, by the looks of it.' I eye the crushed egg-box oozing yellow liquid. 'Ow!'

A sudden pain shoots through my left

ankle. My left arm hurts where I put it out to try and save myself, and because I'm wearing a dress, both my knees are grazed.

'I expect you caught the hem of your dress in the spokes,' Olivia says, as she props my bike against a nearby fence and gathers up my scattered possessions, ramming them back into the basket, minus the eggs.

I make a sound which is half-snarl, half-humourless laugh. Well, I am in pain, and I've made a fool of myself in front of Olivia. *And* she's in my road, facing the direction of the village, which no doubt means she's come fresh from Robin Hill.

'I never have any problem riding my bike in a skirt,' I tell her, more haughtily than I mean to. 'Look, there's a dirty great stone in the road, that's what felled me.'

'Ah, yes.' Olivia walks across and lugs the stone to the opposite verge. 'Let me help you home.'

'I'm absolutely fine, honestly. You go

on.' I nod towards her car, which is not parked in the best position in the narrow road.

But she insists on wheeling my bike around the bend to my front gate while I stand helplessly on the verge before she runs back and gives me her arm to deliver me safely to my front door.

'Your ankle!' she says, as I'm about to thank her and go indoors. 'It's swollen up like a watermelon!'

That's a slight exaggeration but I see what she means. A mouthful of curses mutters its way into the ether. Before I know what's happening. Olivia's taken the key from my hand and is opening my front door. I hobble to the kitchen, trying not to lean on her any more than I have to. I remember inviting her to pop in some time and wonder if I meant it. Well, she's here now, and the kettle's on. I watch her going through the ritual of tea-making while my foot's up on a chair, rapidly turning several robust shades of purple, pink and blue.

I sip my tea — at least she hasn't

insisted I have sugar in it. I hate sugar in tea. I realise she's only made the one cup.

'Do have a drink, Olivia. I've got camomile tea as well as builder's. Or look in the fridge. There's some elderflower fizzy stuff if you fancy that.'

'No, thanks, I'm fine.'

She sits down at the table, watching over me like an anxious parent over a child. Olivia, it transpires, has taken a first aid course. I try not to wince while she tenderly inspects my ankle from all angles, and tests whether I can take any weight on it. I can, just.

'It's a sprain, not a break. You were lucky, but you're going nowhere on this foot for the foreseeable.'

I'm not very good at keeping still. Besides, it's not exactly practical when I live alone. I think these things but don't say them. I don't want to seem ungrateful.

'Ice,' she says, scouting around my kitchen. She opens the freezer and takes out a bag of sweetcorn which she wraps in a tea-towel and lays across my ankle as tenderly as if it were a baby.

'There. Keep that on, and keep the foot up. When I've picked up Anna I'll come back and run you down to the surgery to get it bandaged.'

'No, honestly, you've been marvellous. I've got a friend coming over in an hour or so. She'll take me.'

This isn't true, but all this attention is making me feel claustrophobic, and I've taken up too much of Olivia's time already.

'All right, if you're sure.'

She's taken the hint from my tone that I'd prefer to manage without her now, and I hope I haven't offended her.

'You've been very kind,' I say, forcing a smile through a wall of searing pain. 'I don't know what I'd have done without you.'

I thank her, genuinely, for all her help, gently refuse her offer to bathe my scraped knees, and soon she's at my front door and on her way out. I listen for the door to close, but she ducks back.

'Postman's been.'

A slew of mail lands on the table in front of me. I thank Olivia again, and then she really does leave.

The peace of Sunrise Cottage settles around me. I feel better already. After I've sat and rested for a while, watching the sweetcorn pack drip steadily onto the flagstones, I reach for my phone and look up sprained ankles. Olivia's right; it does need binding up. I think about Max, and then remember he's on an overnighter to a sale somewhere or other. I call Lizzie instead. She's on reception duty at the medical centre at four, she tells me, and immediately arranges to pick me up and take me there before she starts her shift. I can easily get a taxi home again.

I hobble to the sink and swallow a couple of painkillers with a glass of water, then hobble further into the sitting room. Granny Violet's favourite armchair cossets me, and her velvet-topped footstool is the perfect height to rest my foot. I switch on the telly and start to watch a nice undemanding programme about dung beetles. And then I remember my mail which I'd brought through from the kitchen.

All junk. Including the long white envelope with my name and address on a printed label. Yep, that's definitely junk too. I don't know whether it's the shock of the accident and my lucky escape from more serious injury, but I suddenly feel invincible. I don't even bother to open the envelope. Instead, I drop it onto the floor beside my chair. Whoever sent it can go to hell.

★   ★   ★

I'm woken by a storm at three in the morning, which is a nuisance as I've only just dropped off because of the pain in my ankle. Or it seems that way. I go through the childhood ritual of counting the seconds between thunder and lightning. I don't get very far. *One, two* . . . The storm's right overhead.

With the next flash, the bedroom

lights up like a stage set. Fully awake now, I stumble out of bed, wincing as my left foot finds the floor. With difficulty I make my way downstairs, clinging to the banister for support. I remember I had my last painkillers at midnight, so it's too soon for another dose, but I don't fancy going back to bed right away so I make a mug of tea and take it through to the sitting room. My mail is still on the floor by the chair where I left it. The storm must have knocked some sense into me. Switching on the lamp, I pick up the long white envelope and work open the flap with an impatient finger, something I should have done hours ago.

The writer has taken a different approach this time:

I know who you are and what you are.

Who? What? What's that all about, then? My mind, muzzied by pain and the unearthly hour, polkas between not caring and caring very much. It dances between being brave and unafraid to being timid and very afraid. I know now that I have to tell somebody, and I'll do it first thing tomorrow. But who? Max will go into overprotective mode and whisk me off to the nearest cop-shop. He may have a point, but I'll be the one to decide when it's time. My parents? Definitely not. The last thing I want is for them to race hundreds of miles across the country in a sweat, Mum hyperventilating with worry all the way.

I read the note again. It's not even a threat. If somebody was out to get me, physically, they'd make no bones about letting me know, would they? I suppose I could tell Lizzie. She's the most sensible option, the one less likely to fuss. I decide to wait and see how I feel tomorrow.

And so the note makes its way under the clock, with the first two, and I go back to bed.

★　★　★

It's not until four days later that I see Max again. He rang to let me know he was in London for a few days, on business, and there didn't seem any point in telling him about my sprained ankle at the time.

When I open the door to him at seven on Friday evening, his face is a picture of dismay at the state of me — as well as the swollen foot, I'm now decorated with bruises, including a fine specimen on my chin. When I've told him what happened, his shock turns to amusement, and he teases me relentlessly.

'Stop it!' I hang onto the kitchen chair and prod him in the stomach with my free hand. 'You're making me laugh and it hurts!'

'Come here, then.' He holds out his arms and I literally fall into them. 'Let me kiss it better.' And he does, thoroughly.

'I have missed you.' I say, when I'm finally allowed to breathe.

'Missed you more.'

'Nope.'

'Yep.'

We continue with the banal jollities until Max goes back out to his car, and returns with a feast in six brown paper bags.

'I got Chinese, from the one in Little Barton. Good thing, too — I think fish and chips would be too heavy for an invalid, and I won't inflict my cooking on you just yet.'

'That was very thoughtful,' I say.

'Of course it was.'

'I meant about not cooking for me.'

'So did I.'

I laugh. 'Don't let's start all that again.'

We eat in the kitchen, which is my favourite room in the cottage; there's more of Gran about it, somehow. And that's where we remain, until it's properly dark outside and the food's all gone, as well as a bottle and a half of wine.

Max stays over. For the first time. And it's all wonderful, and I'm so happy I can hardly breathe.

* ★ ★

Lizzie rings and offers to contact everyone in the art group to tell them that Tuesday's session is cancelled. She doesn't sound surprised when I tell her I have no intention of cancelling. I've had to pull out of a couple of pub shifts, but I can manage the art easily enough with a bit of help. I'll go stir-crazy if I'm stuck indoors all the time, and I'm without Max's company for a few days. He's off on the trail of a Georgian writing desk he's promised to find for one of his richer clients.

I hear Lizzie sigh at the end of the phone. She knows it's no use arguing. Instead, she says she will collect me, and instructs me that under no circumstances am I to 'lug all that paraphernalia about'.

Everyone rallies round, and in my heightened emotional state, I'm almost tearful as I find myself positioned in the comfiest chair the village hall has to offer, with my foot up on a footstool conjured up out of a cardboard box with a cushion on top, being plied with tea and Marigold's home-made peanut-butter cookies every five minutes. I've brought in a selection of photos of buildings and street scenes, and after I've given a short demo on perspective, my class works happily away.

I stagger round a few times to see how they're getting on, and then when we're finished, everyone rushes to clear up the hall while I sit and wait for Lizzie to run me home.

It's as Lizzie is about to leave my cottage, having made sure I've got everything I need to hand, that I finally decide to be sensible, and I hobble through to the living room and fetch the anonymous notes.

'Violet, this is shocking!' She plumps down on a chair, pushing the bits of paper around on the kitchen table and staring at them with a horrified expression. 'Why haven't you gone to the police? Ooh, I wish you'd told me before. You must be scared witless!'

'Funnily enough, I'm not. Well, I was for a little while. Every bump in the night was a mad axe murderer trying to get in.' I laugh. 'But thinking about it rationally . . . '

'*Rationally?* You can't rationalise this away, surely?'

It's funny, but now I have shared my little problem, I feel the burden of it lifting and the residue of fear is swept away. The trouble with that is that I seem to have offloaded it onto Lizzie, which I'm sorry for.

'It can't be that unusual,' I say. 'Somebody who's lonely, perhaps, and unhappy, losing the plot and doing this sort of thing. I'm the new girl on the block, relatively speaking. Perhaps it's a person who lives in the past, who thinks incomers to the village are the devil's work. My gran lived here for donkey's years. Perhaps they don't like the idea of Sunrise Cottage becoming a second home. It could be that. You know how it is.'

Lizzie narrows her eyes at me.

'You've got this all worked out, haven't you?'

I'm not sure I've got anything in my life *all worked out*, but I nod and smile, before I go to the fridge and take out the wine. I feel in sudden need. I offer Lizzie some.

She looks longingly at the bottle. 'Can't. Driving. Well, go on then, just a tiddly mouthful to keep you company.'

Lizzie has half a glass, I have a full one, and mentally give up on a productive afternoon's painting. I'll read in the garden instead. I am feeling quite tired after this morning's class.

'Violet . . . ' Lizzie looks pointedly at me across the table when she's finished her tiddly mouthful.

'Mmm?' I could do with a sleep now.

'I expect you're right, and whoever's writing these notes has gone cuckoo, poor soul, but why don't you come home with me and stay for a few days? Or as long as you like. I've got a spare room, Sean would be delighted, and the kids won't even notice, not unless you pop up on their mobile phone screens.'

It's such a kind offer, but it's out of the question. I feel completely safe at Sunrise Cottage, I tell Lizzie, as I thank her. I don't tell her I have someone looking out for me here — Granny Violet. I feel that more and more, the longer I stay here, I really do. And now, of course, I have somebody else looking out for me, for different reasons than the notes he knows nothing about, but it means I'm not alone.

Lizzie's face turns a bit pink. She clears her throat. 'Well then, is there any chance you could stay down the road?' She nods vaguely in the direction of the front of the house.

'Down the road? What d'you mean? Oh.'

Lizzie's smiling now. She looks guilty. 'You didn't think you could keep it a secret, did you? About you and Max Finch? Not in a village like Fold.'

I'm struck dumb for a second, and then I burst out laughing. It was stupid, wasn't it, thinking nobody around here would get wind of the situation?

'I didn't like to say anything before,' Lizzie says. 'I gathered you wanted to keep it quiet — and after all, we had been gossiping about him in front of you, which isn't very nice . . . but that's before we knew you were seeing him.'

I shrug. 'It was only gossip. I wasn't seeing him then, anyway. It's a fairly recent development, but it's not serious. It can't be, since I won't always be here.'

Lizzie stands up and takes her empty glass to the sink. 'I'm pleased for you, Violet. Enjoy it while it lasts. I'm sure Max is one of the good guys.'

I can't help spotting the dash of doubt in her voice, and for a second I'm on my guard. And then it passes, and Max's face appears in my mind's eye.

'Yep, he's one of the good guys.'

★   ★   ★

As soon as Max is back, I get my wish to see inside Robin Hill. I like it that he hasn't even unpacked before he drives along to fetch me. I can walk almost normally now, and the swelling's rapidly going down, but it's quite a stretch to Max's and I accept the lift gracefully. Not that I have any choice.

It's six o'clock, and a perfect golden summer's evening. Pink and blue stocks and creamy white nicotiana breathe their sweetness into champagne air as we stroll around Max's lovely garden. He tells me he has a gardener, in the way of a confession, and I tell him truthfully that I'd have one too, if I had a garden of this size.

He laughs. 'Yeah, it's the only way. I just don't have the time. I feel like I'm being pretentious, though, having *staff*.'

Olivia springs to my mind, and for some reason I don't want to think about her right now. She's been very kind, though, like everyone else. Being unable to drive is a nuisance, and Olivia adding my bits of shopping to her supermarket trolley and dropping them round for me has been a godsend.

The spacious rooms of Robin Hill are full of charm and character, as I'd known they would be, and I exclaim over each in turn as Max walks me round as if I'm a prospective buyer. They're also full of furniture and artefacts: many of which, apparently, are actually for sale.

'It's a shame to put it all into storage,' Max says. 'Look at these. Aren't they glorious?' He leads me to where two enormous double-handled vases stand one each side of the wooden Arts and Crafts fireplace in the living room. Exquisitely coloured in reds, blues and greens on a deep yellow background, the vases depict exotic birds and flowers.

'They're Majolica,' Max says.

'I thought so. We . . . I used to see a lot of this kind of thing in Brick Lane and Spitalfields Market. Maybe not as good quality as these. Will they be sold soon?'

'If there's a demand. I might put them in the shop eventually, then I can have a change-around in here.'

I love Robin Hill, and say so, several

times as we go round. Max doesn't show any awkwardness when we reach his bedroom. He opens the door for me to see inside, as if it's any other room. I smile to myself at his choice of bedcover; it doesn't seem like Max. It's a kind of patchwork, large squares of multi-patterned fabric sewn together in random, but very effective, fashion. And then I metaphorically kick myself. Of course it isn't his choice, it's Sarah's. I wonder why he hasn't changed it for something more masculine. But why should he, if he's happy with it?

'Wine time,' Max says, leading me downstairs. 'Let's have a glass out in the garden before we eat. Oh, and don't worry.' He turns round to grin at me. 'I haven't cooked anything. We've got deli stuff and salads. And chocolate pudding for after, ready-made.'

'That sounds lovely, but I wasn't worried. You're probably a very good cook when you need to be.'

'Believe me, I'm not. Sarah would back that up.'

Max grins again, and I like it that he feels he can bring his ex-wife naturally into the conversation when he's with me.

'I've got something to tell you,' I say, as we go into the kitchen.

'Sounds serious.'

'No, not really. It's only that our little *secret* is all round the ruddy village. They know about us — well, Lizzie and her friends do, so no doubt it's common knowledge by now.'

Max isn't perturbed. He laughs, loudly. 'That didn't take long, did it? Well, I don't care. I'm proud to be associated with you, and it means we can turn up in the pub or anywhere we like now, and let the gossips have a field day.'

I sigh with relief that Max is taking it so well. I've decided I don't care either. I've learned from the art group chat that the gossipers rarely mean anything by it. It's almost a hobby, second-guessing what everybody else is up to.

Max doesn't immediately sort out the

drinks, but instead he takes me into his arms and we kiss, and it's a while before we're standing apart, big grins on both our faces. I think about later, and wonder if I'll stay over. Judging by the look in Max's eyes, he's thinking along those lines too. It seems inevitable that I'll stay, and I wonder what happened to my determination not to get too deeply involved. But trying to slow things down now would be like trying to reverse a double-decker bus out of a one-way alley.

Max takes a bottle of wine from the massive American-style fridge and attacks it with the corkscrew. I don't see any glasses so I ask if he wants me to get them out.

'Please. Over there, in the second cupboard.'

Max's kitchen is large, and where there aren't shelves, there are cupboards: tall, handsome cupboards, with grey-painted wooden doors. I take a wild stab at which one he means. No glasses in this one, just crockery. I glance up to the higher shelf, to make sure. Behind me, Max is quietly cursing as the wine cork fails to budge.

I'm about to try the next cupboard when something high up catches my eye. The gold rim of an octagonal cup, more gold rims, turquoise peacock feathers, repeated miniature rural scenes. My Chelsea tea-service.

12

Max couldn't lie to Violet. He thought far too much of her ever to do that. Whatever she needed to know, whatever questions she asked, she'd receive nothing but openness and honesty from him from now on. And so, yes, that was the china he'd bought from her. And, no, he hadn't sold it on.

'Well, obviously, as you've still got it. Silly question,' she'd said. 'I suppose you need to wait for the right time and place to put something so valuable up for auction.'

That wasn't a question, and yet it was. She was curious, as well she might be.

'Is it safe up there, in the top of a kitchen cupboard? Not even wrapped up?'

'Perfectly safe,' he'd said. 'It's also fake.'

'It's what?' Her beautiful blue eyes had regarded him suspiciously. It was clear she hadn't misheard him.

'Fake.'

'I thought that's what you said, but you've got it wrong. That can't be. The Chelsea's a family heirloom — and it's not any old Chelsea, either. It's a fine example, a rare pattern. Max, you said so yourself when I sold it to you.'

He'd shaken his head, spoken gently. 'No, I didn't.'

He could see her mind working, casting back, reaching the conclusion that he was right, he hadn't said any such thing. In fact, he'd hardly said anything at all about the china itself.

'Fake' is probably too strong a word. It's a copy. The Chelsea gold anchor is the most copied of all the porcelain marks because the gold couldn't withstand the heat of the kiln. It had to be painted on top of the glaze, which made it much easier to apply to later pieces.'

'You spotted that straight away, when I showed to you?'

'Yes. But it's a pretty thing in its own right. Nice quality.'

'So it has some value to it?'

'Of course.'

'But not as much as you paid me.'

'There's definitely a market for it, and I will sell it on, when I get round to it . . . '

'But not as much as you paid me.'

'No.'

She'd seemed so far away then, even though she was only on other side of his kitchen. He'd wanted to go to her, hold her close. He tried to close the gap, but as soon as he moved, she'd pushed back, pressing herself against the cupboard door. Then, all at once, she was in front of him, her eyes blazing.

'How *dare* you patronise me like that! What did you think I was? Some sort of charity case?'

'No, of *course* not. Violet, please don't see it like that. There's every chance I can get a good price for it, if and when I decide to sell it on.'

'But you said it was a copy. It's not even Chelsea.'

'No, but . . . '

She'd held up her hands, palms facing him. 'No *buts*, Max.'

He'd fallen silent then. He had no excuses, he couldn't rationalise what he'd done. She was right, he had patronised her, but truly he hadn't meant it that way at the time. He'd figured she wouldn't be selling it if she couldn't do with the money, and he'd seen it as a way to help her. Besides, he hadn't wanted to shatter her faith in the family story about the 'Chelsea'.

He'd got it so wrong. He should have been honest with her from the moment he'd spotted those fake gold anchors, offered her a realistic price, and given her the chance to decline his offer and keep hold of her china.

'How could you even think it was the right thing to do?' There'd been hurt in her voice, as well as accusation.

'I know, it was stupid of me. I made an error of judgement, and I'm so sorry.'

Then, just as he'd thought things couldn't get any worse, she'd faced him with that outdated rubbish about him having done an old lady out of her antiques. How did she know about that? The sour fruits from the village grapevine, he supposed.

This time, Violet had been prepared to listen, and she seemed to believe him when he'd explained that he'd unwisely taken on an assistant whom he knew nothing about, and it was he who'd turned knocker-boy and almost ruined Max's reputation while he was about it.

'I didn't think it could have been anything to do with you, not once I'd got to know you,' Violet had conceded, softening her look. 'But I wanted to hear it from you. You understand, don't you?'

He'd answered her with a swift nod. Suddenly, he realised why she'd brought up that piece of gossip. She'd said she hadn't believed it, yet at the same time she might have wondered whether he'd underpaid her for the so-called Chelsea. It made him angry that she could ever think that of him. But Violet had trust issues. He understood that now, and it

213

wasn't her fault. He only hoped she could find it in her heart to forgive him for the way he'd treated her.

While all this had been going round in his mind, Violet had spoken again.

'Max, I know we may not be together for long, but I still need to know I can trust you implicitly. I've been down that road before, and okay, it's made me suspicious and hypersensitive and protective of myself, but I can't help that.'

'You *can* trust me,' he'd said, 'and I know I can't prove that right now, but give me time and I will.'

Time. The one thing they didn't have. Not enough of it, anyway.

She'd taken some persuading to stay and have a glass of wine and some food. Perhaps he shouldn't have tried to talk her into that, but he couldn't have stood it if she'd left right away. She'd been quiet during the meal, and afterwards, when she said she'd like to go home now, he hadn't demurred.

That was two days ago, and he hadn't heard from her. As he'd dropped her off at Sunrise Cottage, she'd kissed him briefly and said she would phone him, which he'd taken to mean he wasn't to phone her.

Nothing had gone right in the last two days, as if that dreadful evening had triggered off a chain of unpleasant events. The morning after Violet's visit, Olivia had come upstairs to find him in his study, where he'd been staring out of the window, unable to concentrate on anything.

'I'm so sorry, Max,' she'd said, waving a piece of paper at him. 'I was vacuuming and there were papers on the floor, and when I went to pick them up, this was caught under the leg of the chair. I'm afraid it's ripped rather badly. It's such a shame. It's rather good.'

It was a pencil sketch Violet had done of him when they'd been up to Fold Hill. She'd said it was rough and she'd do a proper one of him another time, but he'd jokingly wrestled her for her sketchbook, and in the end she'd torn the page out and let him keep it. He'd asked her to sign it for him. Her first drawing of him. And now it was virtually in shreds. Who knew if there'd be another?

'Don't worry, Olivia,' he'd said. 'It was an accident, easily done. I shouldn't have left it on the floor. Give it here.'

She'd handed it over, apologising again. It was still on his desk. He'd tried to mend it with sticky tape, but not very successfully.

Then yesterday he'd set out for a sale near Hastings that he'd red-ringed in his diary ages ago as a must. Halfway across Sussex in the van, he'd had a tyre blow-out, and by the time the rescue man had turned up, it had been too late to go to the sale and he'd driven all the way home, empty-handed, only to find another one of those anonymous notes among his post.

I said stay away. She's no good for you.

'Like hell I will,' Max muttered to the silent hallway.

This was the second such note he'd received. Whoever was sending them obviously wasn't going to let up. And either they were tracking his movements, adding a sinister twist; or pretending they were, which was almost as bad. He'd vote for the latter. Surely he would have noticed if anyone had been following him or hanging around near Robin Hill or Sunrise Cottage? Well, he'd keep a careful watch from now on.

It was all very well for him, but what about Violet? She had no idea there was somebody out there with a grudge against her — against the pair of them. He longed to see her, partly for his own sake — but, more to the point, he needed to know she was all right.

★ ★ ★

After three worrying days and still no word from Violet, Max couldn't wait any longer. He thought of going to The Rose and Crown on one of her nights, but if he pitched up without warning, he might upset or annoy her more than he had already. He took to driving past Sunrise Cottage slowly, to no avail. Finally, he decided to bite the bullet and phone her on her mobile. At least she'd know it was him, and could dismiss the call if she wanted to.

'Hi Max!' She trilled her greeting into the phone as if everything was fine, and he felt relief wash over him like a warm shower.

'I'm free this evening,' he ventured, after he'd enquired about her sprained ankle and she'd told him it was much better. 'I wondered if you fancied doing something. Dinner at our riverside pub, maybe?'

She didn't speak for what seemed like ages, and then he realised she was talking to someone else in the background.

'Max, I'm sorry,' she said, coming back to him. 'Do you mind if we leave it for a while? Not for long, only I'm really busy with the pub, and I want to finish a new set of watercolour land-scapes to replace the ones I sold.'

She was giving him the brush-off. Letting him down gently. His stomach quaked.

'Violet, we are okay, aren't we? After the other night?' He had to ask, even though he might not like the answer.

'Max, we're fine, honestly. But I am busy, as I said. Sorry, I have to go. I'm standing outside the village hall, just about to start my art class.'

And with that, she ended the call, leaving him slightly mollified but still with the nasty feeling that she was fobbing him off.

★   ★   ★

Max went to Worthing to see Sarah. He'd phoned first, of course, but she greeted his arrival at her flat with effusive delight, as if this was a lovely surprise.

She'd made lunch for him, pasta with clams and shrimps in a cream sauce. It was delicious. He couldn't remember her making it before.

'I'm into fishy things in a big way,' she said. 'I practically live on the stuff these days. It must be because I'm by the sea.'

Max relaxed and enjoyed his meal. Over the years he'd come to recognise the markers of Sarah's state of health and wellbeing, and he had to say that today she seemed fine. Surreptitiously studying his ex-wife across the jazzy-oil-clothed table in her kitchen-diner, he saw a woman in control of her emotions, a woman in charge of her life. He didn't see a troubled writer of anonymous notes.

'In case you were wondering,' she said, dabbing a blob of sauce from her chin with a red-spotted napkin, 'I'm being a good girl and taking my meds. I don't want to end up back at Maytree, thank you very much. I'm far too busy for all that malarkey.'

She laughed. She had a gravelly laugh that he'd always loved when they were a proper couple. He loved it now, but for different reasons.

'Busy doing what?'

'Volunteering. Yeah, I know,' she said, as Max's eyebrows rose. 'Who would've thought it? I give sewing lessons to young people with autism and suchlike. It's about giving them confidence and building their life skills. I try and make it fun for them.'

'I bet you do,' Max said, smiling.

As they chatted, it became apparent that Sarah's own life was being rebuilt too.

'Polly comes round a lot, when she wants to escape from that brood of men she's got at home. And I go over to Mum and Dad's. It's good for me to keep busy, don't you think?'

'Definitely.'

Later, they strolled along the seafront, arm-in-arm like old friends. Max turned the conversation to the village, casually asking if Sarah was still in touch with anyone. She seemed to think that was funny.

'God, no!' She laughed. 'That's all long gone, thank heavens. Why would I be interested in anyone from Fold? Well, apart from you, of course, you old country bumpkin.'

⋆   ⋆   ⋆

Sarah topped up Bronte and Hermione's supper with the last of the clam-and-shrimp pasta and set the bowls down on the floor. Immediately, two sleepy-eyed cats trotted into the kitchen and tucked in.

'I spoil you two,' Sarah said, smiling indulgently.

It had been good to see Max today. He'd looked a bit strained, though, she'd thought. Working too hard, probably.

And what was that all about, asking her if she was still in touch with anyone in that backwater of a village? She'd made a few friendships there in her time, but she could hardly remember their names now, and they certainly wouldn't remember her.

She'd led Max such a dance, hadn't she, with her illness and everything? Too late to do anything about that now. She just hoped he didn't regret having married her in the first place. She certainly didn't regret marrying him. It was all part of life's rich pattern, wasn't it?

He'd marry again one day. Max was the marrying kind. Sarah wasn't sure she was, not any more. He'd have to get his skates on, though, broaden his horizons. A place like Fold was hardly bristling with young single women, was it? She must remember to remind him of that the next time he came.

13

It was true, what I said to Max: I am especially busy at the moment. My watercolour landscapes which were on display in the back room of The Rose and Crown have sold faster than I'd dared hope, and I need to replace them. There's a shop in the village which sells all kinds of decorative items and attracts visitors rather than locals. I got chatting to the woman who owns it, and without any prompting from me, she suggested taking a couple of paintings from me to see how they go.

The long, light evenings bring the punters to the pub to crowd the tables in the garden, and I'm happy to help Fred out by fitting in a couple of extra shifts. At the same time I'm trying to keep my garden in some sort of order, and I've begun painting the kitchen walls in a pale violet colour.

Being busy, of course, isn't the real reason I'm avoiding Max. Having put my doubts about his professional ethics behind me, finding Gran's Chelsea — I'll always think of it as that — languishing in his kitchen cupboard like it was nothing upset me far more than it should have done. He was right, we weren't seeing each other when I sold it to him, but we'd made a connection and he knew that as well as I did. And yet he lied — okay, not directly, but by omission — letting me carry on believing the porcelain was rare and precious, and then paying me well over the odds for it.

After I'd made my discovery I couldn't wait to get home that evening, away from Robin Hill and Max. I needed to clear my head and work out why I was so upset. Max is a good man, I still believe that. He's also human and allowed to make mistakes. God knows I've made enough of them myself. I'm starting to wonder whether, by punishing Max for these small failings, I'm subconsciously punishing Jayden for his much bigger ones. Perhaps, by running away from him, I've missed out some kind of vital stage in the process of dealing with the betrayal and heartache.

Goodness, that's a bit deep, even for me! I don't want to split with Max. Selfish of me though it might be, I want our summer romance to carry on until its natural end. I want to carry on feeling the way Max makes me feel. He brings out the best in me. Even so, after the other night it seems wise to put a little distance between us, dissipate some of the intensity. I thought I might have lost him after the way I reacted, which was scary, until he rang me. I think he understands, though. At least, I hope he does.

But my best intentions to put some space between Max and me are wrecked when, on Saturday morning, the postman delivers another anonymous note.

Stay away from Max Finch if you don't want any trouble.

Now I know that this vendetta, if you can call it that, is nothing to do with my move to the village but with my relationship with Max. The tide has turned. I can't keep this from him any longer.

To my relief, his van and car are both outside Robin Hill when I arrive, breathless from the fast bike ride along Clayfoot Lane. My finger's still fastened to the doorbell when Max is there, a big smile lighting up his handsome face. The smile disappears as he looks at me.

'Violet, what's up? What's happened?'

I launch myself into the hall without waiting to be invited, and find myself restrained by Max's arms circling me. I subside against him, inhaling his warmth and scent like a drowning woman clinging to a life-raft, and I wonder how I ever thought I could keep away from him.

'I thought I'd lost you,' he murmurs into my hair, as he presses closer. 'I'm so sorry about the other night, about everything.'

'I know you are, and I'm sorry I overreacted.' I peel myself away. 'But we have bigger fish to fry now. That's why I've come.'

Max leads me through to the sitting room where I explain about the notes, then take the four envelopes from my bag and show him.

'It's this last one that worries me because it's so specific. Max, this is about you and me, and I don't know why anyone's bothered about us, but it's starting to scare me a bit. And now this clearly involves both of us, I'm scared for you, too.'

Max looks at the strips of paper I've taken out of the envelopes, staying silent. Eventually he stands up and squeezes my shoulder.

'Wait there. I won't be a tick.'

I hear him bounding up the stairs. When he comes back he's holding two white envelopes.

'I got them, too.' He pulls out the

notes and reads them out. 'First one: *Stay away from Sunrise Cottage or you'll be sorry.* Second one: *I said stay away. She's no good for you.* Violet, if I'd known you were being harassed as well, I'd have shared these with you, probably. I didn't know what to do for the best, I only knew I wanted to protect you.' He laughs humourlessly. 'I failed on that score, didn't I?'

It's my turn to fall silent. The messages in Max's notes feel more threatening than mine. They're certainly less cryptic.

'So, any ideas on who our stalker is?' he says.

'Not a clue. You?'

'Nope. I've bandied a couple of names about. This is going to sound really stupid, but I did briefly consider whether it might be your ex.'

'*Jayden?* No way. This is definitely not something he'd waste his time with, and he doesn't know where I am, let alone anything about my life here.'

'Yeah, I know. My daft brain came up

with a proper wild card there. And then I thought of *my* ex, Sarah. It was the scruffy writing that took me there. It doesn't look much like her handwriting, what I remember of it, but Sarah's dyslexic and she has trouble writing neatly and getting the words right. But I know for certain now that it's not her.'

Max tells me about his visit to Worthing, and how he came away convinced that Sarah has nothing to do with this.

We gravitate to the kitchen and Max makes coffee.

'So, do we take this seriously now, or what?' I'm more confused than ever, knowing we've both been targeted.

Max leans against the island, deep in thought. 'I think we need to inform someone, take some advice. Even if this is the work of some sad person who's off their beam, it could lead to something more serious.'

Max says he knows a police officer, somebody at county level. He'll have an unofficial word with him. This sounds a good plan to me, and I feel better already.

Max has to go out shortly, so we leave it at that. It takes me a while to convince him that I'm not afraid of being alone in Sunrise Cottage, which is true, but I promise faithfully I'll ring him immediately if I feel at all uneasy, or anything else happens.

'And you,' I say, picking up my bike from the ground where I'd flung it. 'You take care, too.'

★ ★ ★

It's Tuesday, and I've booked Olivia for another modelling session. She brings Anna, having been let down again on the childcare front, and my students are as pleased to see the little girl as they are our model. Sheila has the idea of drawing Anna as well as her mother, and the others jump at this. So we change our plans a little, and I have Olivia posing on the red sofa, fully clothed. Anna climbs up beside her with the picture books her mother has brought to keep her occupied, and we have an inspiring mother-daughter setup.

Of course, Anna doesn't sit still for long, and soon she's clambering down to run around the hall before she clambers up again, but it's fine. Those who want to draw her have fun trying to capture some kind of image. Olivia is wearing a crinkled cotton ankle-length skirt strewn with pink roses and a tightly-fitting black vest top. She's very drawable, as usual.

'How's the ankle, and the bumps and bruises?' Olivia asks, when we break for coffee and she gets out her bottle of water.

'I'm all mended, apart from a bit of weakness in the ankle, which the nurse says I'm to expect. You were a real star that day, Olivia.'

She laughs. 'I don't know about that. Good to know the first aid course wasn't a total waste of time, though.'

With all the chat at the end of the

session, and the distraction of having a lively two-year-old 'helping' with the clearing-up, I forget to ask Olivia to fill in the claim form for the modelling fees we owe her up until now. I run out of the hall, waving the form, only to see her car vanishing down the high street.

★   ★   ★

It begins to rain later; soft, gentle rain that sweetens the scent from the flowers. I love summer rain, especially after a spell of hot weather. In London, I used to stand on our balcony, absorbing the special, musty aroma that emanated from the pavements. I remember once Jayden coming to see why I was standing in the rain, and when I refused to come indoors, he came out and stood with me, his arms around me from behind, his chin resting on my head.

I remember.

I remember a lot of things about being with Jayden. I guess you can't wipe out the good memories any more than the bad, and why would you want to?

Now I'm on the lawn at Sunrise Cottage, enjoying the sensation of raindrops on my face. The garden welcomes the rain, so I do too. After a while, I feel the dampness seeping into the shoulders of my cotton shirt, and I go indoors to attend to more practical matters, of which Olivia's claim form is the first.

She sounds distracted as she answers her mobile, which I expect is because of Anna. I apologise for having forgotten about the form and explain that it needs to be submitted by the end of this week if she's to be paid on time. She has the solution.

'Will you be home tomorrow at twelve? I could pop in on my way back from Robin Hill.'

'Perfect.'

It's only when we end the call that I realise Olivia probably knows about me and Max, along with everyone else. She may not live in Fold but she spends a good deal of time here, with one thing and another. If there's talk, she'd have picked up on it. I'm not so sure I want her knowing the details of my private life involving her employer. But there's nothing I can do about it, and Max seems to think highly of her, so I have to rely on Olivia being professional enough to be discreet, which I'm sure she is.

★ ★ ★

The following day, I come down from my studio just before twelve. Sure enough, Olivia's car slews to a crooked standstill outside my gate, bang on the dot of midday.

It doesn't take her long to fill out the claim form, which she does hurriedly while bending over my kitchen table. She turns down my offer of a drink as she has to pick up Anna, and she's gone in minutes. I have to plunder my mental reserves to stop myself resenting the fact that Olivia has spent all morning at Robin Hill, possibly with Max there too. Do they make friendly chat in between her domestic duties and Max doing whatever it is he does when he's at home? If so, what do they talk about?

I make myself stop the pointless musings and drop the curtain in the front room window, where I've been standing since Olivia left. Back in the kitchen, I resist the wine and switch the kettle on instead. My coffee on the table in front of me, I reach for Olivia's form, intending to fill in my part and drop it in the post when I go to work at the pub tonight. The pen's in my hand, ready to complete the relevant boxes and add my signature, when a shot of adrenaline blasts through my system and sends me rigid with shock.

I stare at the form, shaking my head as if to clear my eyesight. Then I shove back my chair and run to the other room. Back in the kitchen, I sit down again and compare the writing on the form with that on the threatening notes.

I look at each and every character, matching a slope here, a twist there. Each set of writing has been dashed off without much care for neatness. Each has a letter missing, either squeezed in afterwards or left as it is.

All the evidence points to one indisputable fact: the sender of the malicious notes is Olivia Morton.

★ ★ ★

We seem to gravitate towards high places, Max and I. Geographically speaking, that is. Today we've come to Bramber Castle, which is just a ruin, but it's pretty and romantic and there's nobody here but us. It's Wednesday afternoon, warm but not sunny. A pall of low cloud hangs above us, threatening rain later, but both of us felt the need to go somewhere rather than sitting around in Sunrise Cottage or Robin Hill.

Perched side by side on a piece of broken wall, Max's arm loosely around my shoulders, we gaze across fields and woodland to the blue smudge of the distant horizon. I think we're both still in slight shock, Max especially since he's the one who took it upon himself to deal with the problem.

'I sat her down and made her tell me her story,' he says, continuing the conversation we began in the car. 'I wanted to understand.'

'And do you?'

'Yes, I think so. I did some research on the internet after she'd gone, and what I read made more sense of what's happened to Olivia.'

'Her mother was emotionally distant. That's what you meant when you said she didn't have time for Olivia?'

'Yep. She took care of the basics and that was it. She was there to feed and clothe her and make sure she went to school, but whenever Olivia tried to get close, to give her mum affection, she pushed her away. She never changed, even when Olivia was grown up and forging her own relationships. Olivia said her mother was brought up in a strict household and was never allowed to talk about her feelings. It perpetuates, that kind of upbringing. That's what Olivia puts it down to, anyway.'

'What about the rest of her family? Her father, for instance?'

'She's an only child. Olivia knew her father loved her, but he was a bit of a cold fish too. He was slightly afraid of her mum, and went along with anything she said in order to keep the peace.'

'So both her parents let her down in their own way.'

We lapse into contemplative silence. I think how lucky I am to have parents like mine. Max too comes from a solid, loving family, although sadly his parents aren't around any more.

Earlier, Max had described how Olivia's constant search for a parent figure in her life leads her to form all sorts of unsuitable attachments. Anyone who shows her the least bit of caring, she latches on to. Then she gets incredibly jealous if she sees that person becoming attached to somebody else, in whatever way. I guess it's not surprising that she hasn't had much success with men. Her neediness probably drives them away.

'Max,' I say thoughtfully, 'are you sure it is just this attachment thing and she isn't actually in love with you?'

'She did say she was in love with me, when I first broached the subject.' He gives a little laugh. 'Sorry, it's not funny — I shouldn't make light of it. She kept saying that she could see no other way to be close to me other than to send those notes to try and frighten you away. But then she broke down, and it all came out. She admitted her feelings weren't real, and deep down she's always known that.'

I picture the scene. Olivia arriving at Robin Hill, all set for her morning of domestic duties. Max waylaying her and confronting her with the anonymous mail. She must have been shocked, and probably frightened. But I can't feel pure sympathy for her, not yet. I expect I will in time, but she scared me, and hurt the person she'd formed her latest attachment to, namely Max.

My mind alights on Sarah Finch. How did she deal with all this, I wonder? Did she realise Olivia was becoming attached to Max? But Sarah had her problems too, her own set of demons to face. I doubt it ever occurred to her. Olivia must have hung out the flags when Sarah left and they divorced. I think all this, but I don't say it, nor do I ask any questions. Matters concerning Max's ex-wife are private, and should stay that way.

Max assured me earlier that Olivia is desperately sorry for the trouble she's caused, and she's going to seek help. I sincerely hope she means that, not for mine or Max's sake, but for Anna, her sweet little daughter. I think of Olivia's personality perpetuating, showing up in Anna in later life, and how sad that would be.

Max is thinking about Anna too. 'She's a good mother to that little girl, isn't she? I've always thought so.'

'I'm sure she is,' I say truthfully. 'She's brilliant with her.'

'It's a pity Anna's father didn't stick around long enough to see what a great kid she is.'

I nod. We've talked about this for long enough now. Max gives me a squeeze, which makes me giggle. I suspect it was meant to.

'I'm working tonight,' I say. 'It's ladies' darts night, which means we'll be towering busy. I think I need to go home and have a little lie-down.'

I haven't been sleeping because of all this Olivia business, and it's catching up with me.

'I don't suppose you'd like company? For the lying down part, not the pub part?' Max looks at me and winks.

I smile. 'I could go along with that.'

★   ★   ★

It's only fair that I tell Lizzie who wrote those notes, after I'd confided in her. I know I can trust her to keep it to herself. I have my chance when she comes to the pub that evening to support her cousin who plays in our ladies' darts team.

'No! Not Olivia Morton, surely?' Lizzie places a hand over her heart and looks visibly distressed. 'I can't believe it. She seems such a *nice* person.'

'I know, and she was so helpful to me when I sprained my ankle.'

This is one aspect of the whole business that worries me, the fact that Olivia befriended me to . . . to what? Check on what I was up to? Although she must have been doing that already to know I was friendly with Max. Perhaps she'd spotted him in passing, coming to my cottage — those notes started arriving before I was visiting Robin Hill. Well, however she knew, it's all water under the bridge now. I say as much to Lizzie.

'A false friend! How horrible!' I've given Lizzie a potted explanation about Olivia's reasons for what she did, but she's still outraged on my behalf. 'I hope Max sacked her right away,' she says, eyes blazing.

'He didn't need to. She said she wouldn't be back.'

Max told me he'd paid Olivia a couple of months' salary. I'm not sure I would have. I don't tell Lizzie this. I know what she'd say.

'Naturally she won't show her face in our art class again,' Lizzie says. 'And a good job too!'

'Whose face?'

Too late, I realise Malcolm's come over to where we're having our conflab in the back room of the pub.

'Nobody's,' I say.

'Olivia Morton's,' Lizzie says at precisely the same moment, before she realises her mistake. 'Now, don't go asking why, because you won't be told.'

With no story forthcoming, Malcolm makes up one of his own.

'I said she'd get fed up with stripping off in that perishing hall. Didn't I say so, right from the off?' He looks at us for confirmation, in vain. '*Plus*, she never looked that reliable to me. Oh, yes, you could see that coming a mile off.'

Malcolm rubs his hands together gleefully, like he's been proved right. Lizzie and I look at each other and burst into laughter.

'You're absolutely right, Malcolm,' Lizzie says, patting him on the arm. 'You can't rely on anybody these days.'

★   ★   ★

Max comes in just before last orders. I'd told him not to bother — it's only been a matter of hours since we were together — but I can't help the big grin that spreads across my face as he appears at the bar.

Lizzie has spotted him too, probably before I did, and she's giving me a thumbs-up from her seat in the circle of darts players. Smiling, I shake my head at her.

'What?' Max turns round to see who I'm smiling at, then raises his eyes and orders a pint, and a vodka tonic which is apparently for me.

I didn't cycle down this evening, and Max waits for me outside while I help clear up, then we walk slowly back to Clayfoot Lane in the velvety summer darkness, hand in hand. When we reach the gate of Sunrise Cottage, Max doesn't suggest coming in; I expect I look as tired as I feel. Instead, he looks up at the quarter-moon before he gives me a long goodnight kiss. A kiss that's full of longing, and meaning.

My heart dives. It's the first of August tomorrow. The weeks are racing by, and before long I'll be planning my return to London, ready to pick up my life again. My real life.

'Max . . . ' I look up at him, my hand resting on his chest. 'I don't think we should carry on, the way we have been. It's going to be all the more difficult when . . . at the end of the summer . . . '

His fingertip brushes my cheek and then he takes it away.

'We knew the score from the beginning, didn't we? Enjoy being together while it lasts. Isn't that what we said we'd do?'

'Yes. But that was then.'

'Don't go, then. Stay.' Max's voice brightens like he has the answer to everything. 'Simple, isn't it?'

'That's not part of the plan. You know it isn't.'

'Does there have to be a plan? Can't you just go with the flow?'

I don't have to think about this. 'No. For me, there has to be a plan.'

It's late, we're both tired. Max wisely doesn't continue our conversation.

'I'll call you tomorrow,' he says, kissing me lightly. 'Sleep tight. Oh, and I think there's something you should know.' His voice is serious.

Now what?

'You've got mauve paint in your hair. Night-night!'

14

Jayden Fox leaned both hands on the gate and stared up at Sunrise Cottage, scanning the windows for signs of life. There weren't any. Typical! He'd driven hundreds of miles — not really hundreds, but it seemed like it because he'd taken several wrong turnings — and she wasn't in. He was knackered, and desperate for something to drink. He'd pitched up here fifteen minutes ago, knocked and rung, but to no avail.

He was raging hot, too. It was a warm day, and the apple-green Peugeot he'd borrowed from a mate had no air-con — and no sat-nav, either. Jayden didn't have a car of his own. It wasn't worth it, living in the thick of London. When he needed to go anywhere, he either took a cab or got a friend to drive him. But this was one journey he'd needed to make alone.

Maybe the woman in the post office had got it wrong and there was more than one Sunrise Cottage in Fold. Well, he wasn't going to drive around in a sweat looking for another one. He'd seen a half-decent-looking pub in the village. He could head back there, refresh himself with a nice cold beer, and try again later.

He would have phoned first, had he been in possession of Violet's new mobile number. Or maybe he wouldn't have. It would have spoiled the surprise. He looked again at the windows, with all their curtains half-drawn. Perhaps he'd got it wrong and she wasn't here at all. Or she was here and now she'd gone away. Jayden ran a hot hand across his even hotter head. That would be just his luck.

Then he brightened as he imagined Violet's pretty face, all lit up and smiley with the pleasure of seeing him again, and felt better. Six months, she'd had. More than enough time to calm down, more than enough time to regret her disappearing act. She'd be missing him like crazy by now, but more than likely too afraid to get in touch in case she didn't get a good reception.

Well, he'd solved that little problem for her. If his hunch was right and this was where she'd been living — of course it was right — in a few hours' time or less, she would be back in his arms, and the ring in his pocket would be back on her finger, where it belonged. Then they'd head back to London and pick up right where they'd left off.

She'd have forgotten the business about the paintings he'd copied, and all the nonsense that had followed. All that had died down completely ages ago. The tabloids had said at the time that he'd got away with it. Bloody cheek! He hadn't 'got away with' anything, because he'd done nothing wrong in the first place. It wasn't illegal to copy other artists' work. Just illegal to flog it as the original. Lucky for him things hadn't got that far before some eagle-eyed expert put a spoke in the wheel.

He was too naïve, that was his trouble. Too trusting by half. The fact that he hadn't signed those paintings, because he never did, had been his downfall. How was he to know that by the time they came up for auction, they'd have miraculously acquired the signature of the Spanish painter? Since then, he'd had nothing to do with the little gang of idiots who'd thought they could make a fortune by exploiting his talent.

But he hadn't done so badly out of it in the end. He'd never been in such demand. No, the only casualty there had been his relationship with Violet, and that he was about to rectify.

He didn't imagine for one second that Angelica had anything to do with Violet's flight. Angelica was a decent enough artist, but she hadn't yet tasted real success. She'd looked up to him, seen him as a sort of mentor, and who was he to argue? He liked to help where he could. It was hardly his fault if she was the demonstrative type, prone to throwing herself into his arms — anyone's arms — without warning. There'd been nothing untoward going on there. At least, nothing for Violet to go over the top about, and deep down she knew it. Just a bit of jealousy, that's all it was.

And afterwards, when his days had been lonely, his nights even lonelier, and he'd had no idea what Violet was doing, or who she was doing it with, there'd been no reason to deny himself a spot of comfort when it was handed to him on a plate. Violet didn't need to know about that, of course. It would only confuse things.

So, here he was, all ready to forgive and forget. *But where was Violet?*

Jayden got back into the Peugeot and sat for a minute, drumming his fingers on the dashboard, before he made a tight three-point turn, cursing the narrowness of the lane, and set off back to the village with a diesel roar.

* ★ *

I've just had an anxious moment. I almost bumped into Olivia. Not that I have anything to fear from her now; never did have, had I but known it. But I really don't want to see her any more, let alone talk to her. That would be awkward in the extreme. After my art class, I nipped along to the post office to send a parcel to Mum for her birthday, and as I came out, I saw Olivia pushing Anna along in her buggy on the opposite side of the street.

It's not a very wide road, and I'm sure she must have seen me, but she obviously doesn't want to bump into me, either, and she hurried on past without acknowledging me. I think she's leaving the area. I don't know for certain, but I was driving along the Little Barton Road yesterday, and there was a 'For Rent' sign up on the cottage I think is hers. It might be silly of me, but I feel guilty. It seems a shame for her to uproot herself, and little Anna, when she has her life here. Well, wherever she goes, I hope she finds happiness, and manages to sort herself out.

I stand on the pavement for a moment, watching Olivia's elegant figure receding into the distance, then decide to call in to the shop where some of my pictures are displayed. Wendy, the owner, almost falls on me as I walk in.

'I'm glad you came,' she says. 'I've been meaning to get in touch but I've not had a sec to spare. Those sketches you did of the view from Fold Hill have gone down a storm: I've only got one left, and just two of the watercolours. Can you fetch in some more?'

The sketches she means are the drawings I did using soluble pen, then washing a little colour in afterwards. The smudgy effect is very effective, and I was pleased with the way they'd turned out. So, apparently, were the customers at Wendy's lovely shop.

'Ooh, that's good. I've got a couple

more sketches. I'll frame them up and bring them in. The watercolours might take a bit longer.'

Those are selling well in the pub, and I've promised Fred another couple too.

'Fantastic,' Wendy says. 'I'll up the price a bit, shall I? It's summer, people are on holiday. They won't mind forking out a bit extra, and they're well worth it.'

Since my visit to the ruins of Bramber Castle with Max, I've been back there on my own, made some sketches and taken a lot of photos. The pen-and-wash medium will work well for that. Wendy says she'd love to take some of those as well, and I'm practically dancing by the time I leave the shop. I'm going to have to work my socks off, but that's fine. I love my art more than ever, now that I have the countryside at my elbow. I feel so lucky to be getting paid for doing something I enjoy.

As I stroll back to my car, which is parked outside the village hall, I meet

Malcolm coming out of the little supermarket, weighed down not only by a rucksack full of his art equipment, but three full carrier bags of shopping as well. I offer him a lift home but he says he's fine, he only lives five minutes away.

'Tell you what, though, Violet,' he says, 'I'll be thankful to get home in one piece.'

'Oh, why's that, then?'

'Prat in a green Peugeot nearly ran me down when I was crossing. He was going so fast I wouldn't have stood a chance if I hadn't jumped the last bit. *Plus* the exhaust was positively belching. Made one hell of a racket in our nice quiet street.'

Fold high street's not that quiet, there's plenty of through traffic on a weekday, but we can do without boy racers. I agree with Malcolm there.

'Well, you take care the rest of the way home,' I tell him.

Once I'm in the car, I think about all the jobs waiting for me at Sunrise

Cottage. My new bedroom curtains need putting up before the old ones disintegrate altogether, I've still got two walls of the kitchen to paint, I haven't run the vacuum round for a week, and I can hardly see out of the back window for honeysuckle. And that's before I've begun on my paintings. But it's a gorgeous golden day, warm but fresh, unlike the debilitating heat we had a couple of weeks ago, and it's great to be outdoors. Sunrise Cottage, bless its heart, will still be there when I get back.

I check my phone before I start up, and there's a short text from Max simply saying 'Hello', with a heart and a kiss on the end. I won't be seeing him for a few days as he's up to his eyes, as he puts it, and will be on the road a lot. With a smile on my face, I text back in a similar vein, then I wind down the car window and set off in the opposite direction from Clayfoot Lane, with no particular destination in mind.

As I draw level with The Rose and Crown, I notice a green Peugeot in the car park, which is probably the one Malcolm was complaining about. I'm working tonight, but I'm not sure which other evenings Fred wants me this week. For a moment I consider nipping into the pub to see him, and I slow down. But then I change my mind and drive straight on. I'll find out about my shifts soon enough.

★   ★   ★

It's half past four by the time I'm back in Fold, later than I'd planned, but I've thoroughly enjoyed playing truant.

When I drove out of the village this morning, I kept going until I reached the coast, enjoying the feel of the sun and breeze on my face, and the freedom to take the day as it comes. I ate a delicious crab salad for lunch at a beachside café buzzing with holiday-makers, then I walked, quite a long way, past beach huts painted in cupcake colours, until I reached the sand-dunes, where there were few people apart from the occasional dog-walker.

My sketch pad goes with me everywhere, and soon my pencil was flowing around the gentle curves of the dunes, echoing the indolent sweep of the waves. And then I found myself idly drawing Sunrise Cottage, and wondering how it will get on without me. I don't know how I'm going to keep the garden and everything under control once I'm back living and working in London. My mind has been occupied with this during the journey back. I could rent the cottage out, but somehow I don't like the idea of strangers living in Granny Violet's home. I guess I shall have to employ somebody to keep the garden down, at least. Perhaps Max's gardener will take it on, if I can afford him.

Max, and my confusion over my feelings for him — yes, I admit I am confused — still occupy the centre of my mind as I drive along Clayfoot Lane. And there's that car again, the Peugeot, and it's right outside Sunrise

Cottage. I slow down and let my car creep the last few hundred yards, a frown etched deep on my forehead.

I'm right up close to the Peugeot before I realise. Its door swings open and he's there, standing by my car, one hand on the door handle, a broad, confident grin on his face.

'At last!' Jayden says. 'I was starting to give up hope.'

15

'What are *you* doing here?'

I climb out of my car. Not easy with no feeling in my legs.

'That's a nice welcome. You *are* pleased to see me?'

Jayden holds his arms open. Automatically, I take a step back.

'Aw, Violet, don't be like that.' He leans in to kiss me on the cheek.

The contact throws my head into a spin. I clutch the gatepost to steady myself.

'Stop it! How the hell did you find me, Jayden? And *why*?'

'Why d'you think?' His eyes widen. 'Cool cottage, by the way. It was hard to find. I thought it would be in the actual village, not halfway down a track.'

'Clayfoot Lane is *not* a track,' I say, glaring at him.

Why am I defending where I live? He's already got me on the back foot, and he hasn't answered my first question. I think about Max. I don't know when he's due home, but supposing he drives past right now and sees me with Jayden?

'You'd better come in.' I walk up the path, keys in hand, Jayden following. I lead the way to the kitchen. 'Don't get too comfortable. You aren't staying.'

Even as I say it, I know that whatever comes next isn't going to be easily dealt with. It's going to take time.

I want to make tea, let the ritual of kettle-filling and mug-tinkering calm me down. But Jayden doesn't want tea. He goes straight to the sink as if it's his own, takes a mug down off the hook and fills it with water, downing it in one.

'That's better. I had a terrible thirst. Is there anything to eat going?'

'Never mind that. How did you find me?'

'Can't we leave the technical details

262

till later?' Jayden appraises me, then smiles. 'You're a sight for sore eyes, Vi.'

★   ★   ★

The next half an hour passes in a daze. I feel as if I'm walking through a dream. It's as if I'm seeing myself from a distance, like a character in a play. A really bad play. A play about somebody else's life, not mine. I watch myself sliding rashers of bacon under the grill, cracking the last of the farm eggs into the frying pan, slicing bread for toast. I put out cutlery and we eat, mainly in silence. Jayden looks ravenous, as if he hasn't eaten all day. He was like that before. He'd be so absorbed in his work that he wouldn't stop, and I'd have to prise him from his studio like a mussel from its shell, then he'd eat like a starving man. Like he does now.

I remember this as if it was yesterday. My unwary mind brings back this detail and I'm shocked to find that it hurts. It really does.

'How have you been?' I ask, when eventually he puts his fork down.

'It's been strange, without you.'

I nod. 'I had to do it. I'd have gone crazy, in that apartment . . . '

Jayden's mind fills in the rest. 'You weren't on your own, Vi.'

'Yes, I was. Even when you were there. I should have ended it, long before. I knew, deep down, we'd lost us.'

It sounds banal, clichéd, but it's the best I can do for now. I'm still reeling from Jayden having turned up out of the blue and I'm not up to any deep discussions. In any case, there's no point. I tell Jayden this.

'It's okay,' he says. 'We don't need to discuss anything. No point in raking up the past. I haven't come here for that.'

'Then why have you come?'

'To take you home, of course.'

I stare across the table. 'Take me *home*? Jayden, I ran away, and stayed away, for six months. I didn't leave an address or contact you, I changed my phone number, I changed my *life*. Does that not tell you something?'

'You needed time out, a break. Yep, I get that.'

I sigh with frustration. 'I also left my engagement ring behind, remember?'

'Ah yes, that.' Jayden wriggles a hand into the pocket of his tight jeans and holds up the ring. 'Here.'

This is so ridiculous I almost laugh. I would if I wasn't too busy trying not to cry. I push back from the table and go to stand up, but somehow I don't quite make it and I drop back onto the chair.

'Jayden, I can't handle this. I don't know where your head's been these past months, but obviously you've been under the illusion that we've been biding time, waiting for the moment when we get back together. *Why?* Why would you think that? If I'd wanted a break, as you put it, I'd have said so. I wouldn't have done a runner, would I?'

Jayden returns the ring to his pocket and looks at me, long and hard, before his shoulders slump. He stares down at the table, silent, brooding. When, after a minute, he looks up, I see something different, something less demanding, less sure. It was all bluster, pretending we've been on a break and now it's time to go home. He's known all along what my intentions were, that snowy February day. And now he's come to try and win me back, and he has no idea how to go about it.

'Oh, Jayden.' It comes out as a whisper.

'I love you, babe. Honest, I do. I don't want to be without you, not any more.'

'How did you find me? You never said.'

'You left a lot of stuff behind. Drawers full of papers and things. I was looking through and I found a photo. An old black-and-white one, of this place. On the back it said *Sunrise Cottage, Fold, Sussex.* There was a date, nineteen-fifty-something. And then I remembered your inheritance, and I knew where to find you. We never did come here together, did we? Always too busy, I guess.'

Actually, I never asked Jayden to come down here with me. I'd wanted to see Sunrise Cottage alone after Granny Violet died. It felt private, too personal to share with anyone. That was my mistake. I know that now. I should have shared it with Jayden. We were, after all, supposed to be spending the rest of our lives together.

'I'm sorry,' I say. But I don't say what I'm sorry about, and the words hang in the air between us like an unsolved crossword clue.

'Jayden, why did you wait this long before you came looking for me?'

'I only found the photo last week.'

He looks a bit shamefaced. He can't look at me. The penny drops.

'You had no *intention* of finding me before that, did you? You found that photo and thought, ah, that's where she must be. I think I'll drive down, oh, and while I'm there, I'll see if I can get her to come back.'

He doesn't agree but neither does he deny it.

'I've been lonely. I've really missed you, Vi. Look, pack a bag and we can be home inside an hour if I put my foot down.' He smiles brightly, his eyes full of hope.

'I *am* home,' I say, quietly. And it's as if I'm saying it to myself.

There's no way in the world I'm going to admit to Jayden that I'm going back to London at the end of the summer anyway. He would latch on to that and use it to further his cause.

I look at my watch. I'm due at work in precisely twenty minutes.

'You work in a pub?' Jayden says, when I tell him. 'That's a turn-up for the books.'

'Yes, well, I enjoy it.' And there I go again, justifying myself when I have no need to. 'When I get back, I want you gone. Understand? Do what you need to do, make a drink or something, use the bathroom, whatever, then please leave, and make sure the front door's shut properly.'

Jayden nods. It's all I'm going to get.

All I've got time for. I fly upstairs and change. Ten minutes later, I'm in the car; it's too late to cycle or walk.

★   ★   ★

I give the wrong change twice, vodka instead of gin once, drop and smash three glasses as I'm collecting them. Fred and Doreen raise a metaphorical collective eyebrow but don't pass comment.

Damn Jayden! Why couldn't he have stayed away, respected my decision? It also enters my mind that perhaps I went about it the wrong way, and we should have sat down and talked it all through, then said a proper goodbye, which would have been the inevitable end. At the very least I could have left a note, or written a letter afterwards. I wonder how I would have felt if it were me, abandoned without a word? Was I unkind to him? Or was I being cruel to be kind?

These thoughts circulate in my brain

throughout the whole of my shift. Not only that, my eye is constantly on the door, half-hoping, half-dreading, that Max will walk in. He doesn't, and I realise I'm glad. It would be too much to cope with all at once.

Despite my shock and unease at seeing Jayden again, a memory is triggered of how our life was — before success and all the trimmings went to Jayden's head and left me wondering what happened to the man I fell in love with. He has a wonderful talent, and I'll always admire him for that. The vigorous, colourful canvases became must-haves for collectors of contemporary art and celebrities alike, and I celebrated that along with him. I can hear him now. 'One day I'll be in the Tate Modern, Vi.'

And he will.

Lizzie and Sean come in to the pub, and I'm so pleased to see somebody I can talk to, I almost burst into tears. Fred lets me take my break, Lizzie abandons her husband and we head to a corner of the back room. Lizzie knows a little about my life before I arrived in Fold but not the whole story. She hears it now.

'I don't go much for modern art, and I can't pretend I've heard of Jayden Fox,' she says. 'I think I might have seen him today, though. Tall, dark guy, bit of a Heathcliff with added embellishments?' She taps the side of her nose, and her earlobe, referencing Jayden's nose-stud and single earring.

'Yep, that's the one.'

'I saw him hanging about the high street as I was on my way home from our class. Stuck out like a sore thumb. I'm surprised you didn't see him yourself.'

'I must have just missed him. The first I knew was when I found him outside my cottage this afternoon.'

I don't have to over-explain to Lizzie. She's right there, on the spot.

'I take it he's not come all this way just to pass the time of day.'

'Nope.'

'Could you ever go back, try and find

what you had before, with Jayden?'

'No, I don't love him any more, not in the way I used to, and he doesn't love me, despite what he claims. We aren't a good fit. I've grown out of that kind of life, whereas Jayden never will.'

'And Max Finch?' Lizzie says quietly. 'Where does he fit in?'

'Max? I'm not sure he fits in anywhere.' I laugh ruefully.

'Violet, I've seen your face when you mention him, and I've sensed you becoming happier the longer you're in the village. I don't think that's just down to a pretty cottage and a few art classes, is it?'

I sigh. 'You're right, of course. But what's the point? I'll be leaving in a matter of weeks.'

Lizzie gives me a sideways look. 'So you keep saying.'

★   ★   ★

At the end of a very long night, I arrive home to find that the green Peugeot hasn't moved. And neither has Jayden. He's made it as far as my sofa, and that's it. I'm so exhausted, physically and mentally, that I can't find it in myself to feel either surprised or angry.

I fetch a blanket from upstairs and drape it over his gently snoring form. The curtains aren't drawn. The moon douses his face in a pale, watery light and throws into relief the ludicrous curl of his long black eyelashes. I used to rib him about those eyelashes, tell him they belonged on a girl. And when he fell asleep before me, I would prop up my head on my elbow and look at them for ages.

Asleep, Jayden reverts to the man I once loved to distraction.

My heart remembers, my body remembers.

Muscle memory, that's all.

★ ★ ★

'I never cheated on you, Vi,' Jayden says, spreading crumbs far and wide as the last of the bread makes its way into the toaster. He seems to be on his second breakfast. 'I know what you thought about me and Angelica, but she's not my type. Didn't go near then. Don't now.'

I sit down at the kitchen table. Jayden pushes the butter towards me, as if I'm the guest.

'What do you mean, you don't *now*?'

I'm confused. Jayden's spent the last ten minutes describing his present life; in which, apparently, he works even harder than before, plays a lot less, and moves in different, less frantic, social circles.

'She's still around, obviously. We go to the same gigs. Can hardly block her, can I, babe?'

'That's not what I meant. Jayden, I don't care what you do or who you associate with. You brought Angelica up, not me. But I'd rather you didn't make out you're living some kind of monastic life just to impress me because, believe me, it doesn't.'

Jayden comes round to the back of my chair, puts his arms round my shoulders and drops a kiss on the top of my head. His closeness disturbs me. I'm touched by his presence, and oh, how I wish I wasn't.

'*Don't*, Jay.'

Immediately he backs off. 'There's still something there, between us, Vi. You know it as well as I do. We can build on that, start again. Say you'll at least think about it?'

I hear him but I don't turn to look at him. I need a second to regroup, remember how miserable I was, and that leaving Jayden was the best decision for both of us.

He clatters our breakfast things into the sink, splashes hot water on them, then turns round and looks questioningly at me.

'Give it up, Jayden. We don't belong together, and deep down you know it.' I smile, and glance pointedly at the clock. 'You should get going.'

It's another half an hour before I

finally manage to manoeuvre Jayden out of my front door and into his car. He tried again to win me round. Of course he did — I'd expected nothing less. I gave him my new mobile number. He wrote down the full address of Sunrise Cottage and promised to send me an invitation to the exhibition he's showing at in the autumn. We even shared a hug.

His last words were, 'I'm not giving up on you, Vi. There'll never be anyone else. I'm crazy about you, and I'd marry you tomorrow if you'd let me.'

Well, I thought those were his last words. I'm upstairs in my studio, deciding which of my landscapes to work on today — I need the distraction of painting — when the door bell rings. Immediately I think of Max, and I sprint across the landing to my bedroom, fling the window open and look down.

Jayden looks up, shading his eyes. 'Don't know of a mechanic round here, do you?'

And then I see the tail-end of the silent green Peugeot, just visible at the bend in the lane.

16

Max didn't need Violet to tell him that Jayden Fox was in Fold. He'd heard it in The Rose and Crown when he took Oscar there for lunch. Oscar was an old friend who was passing through on his way to a business meeting, and the two of them were at the bar when somebody mentioned the 'artist type' who'd been asking where Sunrise Cottage was. A colourful description had followed, and Max could only assume they were talking about Violet's ex.

When Violet rang him that evening with this unwelcome piece of news, he'd just said, 'I know', and she'd let out a big sigh and said, half to herself, 'Is nothing private in this village?'

'It's fine. You do what you need to do, and I'll see you when you can,' he'd told her, thinking it was anything but fine.

What was the man doing here? Violet had said he'd turned up unannounced, and she wouldn't lie, but it could only mean one thing: Jayden wanted Violet back. He'd hardly drop in for a chat after six months of absence from her life, would he? He hadn't questioned her — it wasn't as if he and Violet were in a committed relationship, regretfully, and it was none of his business. But she had said she'd explain if he wanted to call in at the pub on Friday night.

An old green Peugeot had been parked crookedly in Clayfoot Lane, on the tiny bit of grass verge just along from Violet's cottage, for several days now. He'd been wondering whose it was, and now he knew exactly who the vehicle with the 'broken down' cardboard sign stuck on the windscreen belonged to. Max snarled at it as he walked by on his way to the pub. He would have kicked its tyres, if it wouldn't have been way too childish. How long did it take to get a car fixed, for goodness sake? He couldn't be trying very hard, could he? Which was another cause for alarm.

Max had considered giving the pub a miss, but it might seem as if he was sulking. In any case, he wanted to hear what Violet had to say, even if it heralded gloomy news for him.

He bought her a drink, and they chatted across the bar as usual, before he sat down at a table near the door to wait for closing time and her shift to end. She seemed okay; happy to see him, perhaps happier than usual, which gladdened his heart. But she was on duty and it was a barperson's job to be cheerful. He just hoped the sweet smile she'd given him and was currently sharing among the punters wasn't the same smile which greeted Jayden Fox first thing in the morning. Speaking of which, where was he sleeping? There was only one bed in Sunrise Cottage, and that was Violet's.

Max decided to push these negative thoughts aside. Hadn't she warned him not to get too involved with her? It was hardly her fault if he'd let his emotions run away with him. The thing was, he had the impression that she wasn't exactly immune herself, giving him hope that their summer fling — holiday romance, or whatever it was — could easily develop into something more.

By the time Violet was ready to leave, he'd worked his mood up into something close to upbeat. He kissed her as soon as they were outside the pub, and they held hands like teenage sweethearts as they walked along the high street towards the turning which led to Clayfoot Lane.

'I'm glad you came,' she said, after a worrying silence. 'Sorry I've not been around much.'

'Understandable.'

'Oh, Max.' Violet suddenly stood still and threw her arms round him. 'I'm going to miss you *so* much. I would say we should keep in touch, but that wouldn't be right.'

'Wouldn't it? Who wouldn't it be right for, exactly?'

'You. Me. Oh God, I don't know. I can't think straight, and that's because I seem to be stuck with Jayden. He refuses to go home by train. He told me he'd rung a garage and organised a mechanic to come out, but now he says they haven't got parts for that make of car. I don't think he's rung them at all.'

Max gently extricated himself from Violet's arms. 'Missing me, and Jayden being here, are all part of the same dialogue, then.'

'He wants me back. I'm not *going* back. To London, yes, but not to him.'

'Are you sure about that? Jayden, I mean?'

'Totally. The only feelings I've got left for him are the nostalgic sort. But every minute he stays reminds me that I had — *have* — a good life in London. It may be noisy and crowded and expensive, and if I do get a waft of air it's not scented with grass and sun-shine, it smells of something foul and comes out of the mouth of the Tube. But I've lived there for ten years and it's home. Besides, the schools and colleges will be recruiting soon, ready for September. There are people I need to see before they forget about me altogether.'

That was quite a speech. Max wondered who she was trying to convince, him or herself.

'Violet, are you saying you may go back to London sooner rather than later?'

'I think it would be for the best.'

★   ★   ★

He hadn't argued with her, nor tried to persuade her that she could have a good life in Sussex. Okay, it wouldn't be as fast-paced, and there wouldn't be the range of opportunities there were in London; but she'd seemed so settled, so content in her gran's cottage, with her work and her new friends. From the first day he'd met her, when she'd been painting in the middle of a field, he'd watched her lose the city pallor, the faint droop of her shoulders, the wary look in those blue eyes, the anxious downturn of her mouth. Violet had blossomed before his eyes, and if that was a sight to be denied him in future, he wasn't sure he could bear it.

But when they'd reached Clayfoot Lane, he'd kissed her goodnight and let her go without a word. It was her decision.

Now it was Saturday morning, and the weekend stretched ahead. He had no work commitments, nothing planned. He'd hoped to see Violet. He didn't see why she couldn't leave Jayden on his own for a few hours, if she hadn't managed to get shot of him by now. But, of course, it wouldn't just be about her stubborn house-guest. It would be about her deciding where her life was heading next, and she didn't need him getting in the way of that.

Max opened the back door and strode up the sloping lawn to the top of his garden. From there, if he stood at a certain vantage point, he could see the chimney of Sunrise Cottage through the trees. Feeling like some kind of stalker, he shaded his eyes to stare in that direction, as if by concentrating hard enough he could divine what was going on beneath its roof. He couldn't, of course.

But there. It was pointless driving himself mad, wondering if, and when, she would pack up and leave. Violet was moving on, getting on with her life. Perhaps it was time for him to move on, too, and start again, somewhere new. All the pointers were there, including something which had happened last week.

Sarah had rung and asked if she could see him whenever it was convenient. Since he had business in Chichester the following day, it was no trouble to make a detour to Worthing on the way home.

She looked well, even better than the last time. The cruel illness would never go away completely, but now, instead of fighting it, she seemed to be making allowances, taking real care of herself, and there was no reason why she shouldn't stay well for a very long time.

'So,' she'd said, poking him jokily in the chest, 'you don't need to worry about me any longer. Not that you ever should've done. I've got something to show you. Come on.'

She'd frogmarched him out of the flat, down the road, and around a couple of corners, to a small shopping parade. One of the shops, selling flowers, had a 'For Sale' board tacked to its upper regions.

'Flowers.'

'Flowers now. But I see it as an art and craft shop, selling everything you'd need to make things and be creative. I might even call it *Arts and Crafts*, like Robin Hill. Appropriate, don't you think?'

'Yes, but . . . '

'Max, this is why I asked if you could come. Before, I had no need of any money from our house, but I've had a bit of a re-think, and now . . . '

'You want to buy this shop.'

'I do. I need something to get my teeth into, as well as the volunteer work. I can't swan up and down Worthing seafront like an OAP for the rest of my life. But if this is in any way a problem, then you *must* say. Promise you'll say.'

Max grinned. 'I promise.'

'I'd still prefer you to have the whole damn house, but I know you're not comfortable about it, so . . .'

Max's grin widened. It was the perfect solution. He was so glad Sarah had finally seen sense and agreed to take her share, and that she was so excited about her plans for the future.

'I assume you can't afford to buy me out,' she said. 'So it looks like we're selling up. Mum and Dad will lend me the money to buy the shop, and I'll pay them back out of the house sale, so there's no hurry. Take a year — longer, if you like. My parents are fine with it.'

No hurry.

No reason to hang about, either.

Max sent an air-kiss spiralling on the

breeze in the direction of Sunrise Cottage before he marched back down the garden and went indoors. Twenty minutes later, he'd made appointments for three estate agents to come and value the house.

17

Sunday. The Peugeot finally got fixed yesterday evening and Sunrise Cottage is down to one occupant. *Please God, let it stay that way,* I pray to the ceiling as I collect used coffee mugs from random places, scrub the ring off the bath and vacuum up the crumbs. I was the one who kept the Brick Lane apartment clean and tidy, in spite of Jayden's immense pride in it. I wonder what kind of a state it's in these days.

As I plump up the sofa cushions, flattened by their overuse as a bed and general flop-house, I amuse myself with wild imaginings as to what it would be like if Jayden lived here, with me. Nightmarish. Improbable. Not going to happen. Ever.

This suggestion was his last-ditch stand, as he turned over the car's uncertain-sounding engine. If I really wanted to live in the country so badly, he could go along with that, oh yes. We'd live here and he would commute to London, stay overnight in the apartment when he needed to, and everything would be rosy. This would be after we'd had the wedding I'd apparently always dreamed about.

The whole ridiculous scenario roughly translates into me in Fold and Jayden in London, shackled to each other like anchors to the sea-bed with nothing going for us but frantic conjugal visits whenever it suited. Perhaps he wouldn't make it as far as Sussex on those occasions, and we'd meet half-way at a Travelodge off the motorway.

I'm still laughing to myself as I trundle off to the village on my bike with no particular purpose in mind. Well, it helps to take my mind off Max Finch.

As I turn the corner and enter the high street, I'm greeted by several waves and cheerful 'Hello's as people I know, some only by sight, pass by on the pavement. Kevin drives past with his wife in their four-by-four, and gives me a merry double-toot. All this makes me feel warm inside. The friendliness of this little community is something else I'll miss when I'm back in London.

I haven't bothered with newspapers since I came down here. I catch up with the news on TV and the internet, and the rest of the rubbish they print I don't need. But as I pass the newsagent's, the racks stuffed with fat Sunday papers catch my eye, and on impulse I stop off and buy one. I wheel the bike further along the pavement and padlock it to the metal bar, then take my paper into Cherry on the Top to enjoy a leisurely coffee and a read.

I order an almond croissant with my coffee. I recognise the teenage girl who brings it over. She's a sixth-former at the comprehensive where I helped with the Saturday art club last term. As she realises who I am, she sits down at my table and tells me she's thinking of applying to art college after her exams next year, and which ones do I think are the best? After we've had a chat, and she goes off to serve somebody else, it occurs to me that I could be useful in Fold, as much as anywhere. I don't go as far as thinking I'm needed — that sounds as if I'm full of myself, which I'm not — but my Sunday-morning outing has triggered something in me, something I'm trying to catch hold of and pin down, just for a moment, so that I can examine it more closely and understand it. Like a child catching a butterfly in a net before setting it free.

I scoop the remains of the froth from inside my coffee cup and spoon it into my mouth, my mind caught up in a whirl of thought. I feel as though I'm on the edge of some kind of epiphany.

I pedal home faster than I did on the outward journey. Sunrise Cottage seems to smile as I approach the blue front door. It's only the full beam of the midday sun gleaming on the windows, but knowing that doesn't lessen the welcoming effect. Inside, I stand in the middle of the kitchen, wishing Gran could see how fresh it looks with its pale violet walls and sparkling white window frames. I've hung one of the embroidered pictures of violets in here, on the wall that receives the least direct light, in case it fades.

A long-ago visit to Gran's, with Mum and Dad, comes into my mind. I must have been about eight. There were many such visits, but this one stands out in my mind because of the rabbits. We'd been for a walk along Clayfoot Lane and down one of the tiny turnings leading from it, and there were rabbits scampering around a field. I was transfixed, and stood by the fence for ages, watching them, not moving, and being ever so quiet, otherwise they'd get scared and run away, Dad said.

Then later, when we sat down to dinner, it was rabbit pie. I burst into tears and refused point-blank to eat any, citing the sweet little bunnies running round the field. I don't remember much more about it. I know a lot of pacifying went on, but whether

I ate the pie in the end I have no idea. I do remember tea-time, though. Not necessarily that day: tea-times at Sunrise Cottage are all rolled into one memory, but they had one thing in common.

Leaving the kitchen, I go into the living room, open the tall cupboard and take out a white porcelain cup and saucer, hand-painted with violets. Not only did Gran bring out the set for visitors, she used it every day. Precious though it was, Gran didn't believe in sentiment. She believed in putting things to their proper use.

I reach into the cupboard and bring out some of the china and then, although I've not long had coffee, I make myself a pot of tea, using the violet-strewn teapot and cup and saucer, and the matching jug for the milk. Even with my usual tea-bags instead of the loose tea Granny Violet used, it tastes wonderful.

I sit in the kitchen, smiling into the sunlight and cradling the empty cup, and it's a while before I remember the newspaper I bought and didn't get round to opening. It's in my bicycle basket, and I fetch it and spread it on the table. I'm flicking through the pages without much interest, when I come across a column of gossipy tit-bits about so-called famous people. C-list doesn't even come close. I'm about to turn the page when Jayden's name leaps from the endmost item:

Visitors to an open-air exhibition of contemporary art in London's Hyde Park last weekend were treated to a display of histrionics when an up-and-coming artist known only as Angelica confronted talented dauber Jayden Fox, accusing him of having an affair with gallery assistant Elsa Bain. Angelica's on-off relationship with Fox became serious after she moved into Fox's desirable Brick Lane residence, two months after a former girlfriend is believed to have left. Fox was not available for comment.

Carefully, as if I'm nursing an injury, I stand up from the table and take my cup and saucer to the sink. Carefully, I wash it, rinse out the tea pot and milk jug. Carefully, I dry them, and set them aside, ready to use again. Only when I've completed this task do I allow myself to think about what I've just read.

That Jayden's been seeing Angelica — living with her, in fact — is hardly a surprise, nor that he's apparently betrayed her too. As I told him, he's free to do as he likes, has been since I ended it by walking out, and I don't care about any of that.

What I do care about is the big fat lie he told me only days ago, when he'd made a special point of telling me he wasn't seeing Angelica, and never had been. This statement was presumably made in case I'd got wind of the affair, which wouldn't exactly further his cause.

The reality was that Jayden had been dumped, publicly at that, whether it was true about his other affair or not. His pride had been hurt — probably not much else — and he'd removed himself from the firing line and come racing down to Sussex. What better way to get himself out of trouble than to reignite his relationship with his long-term girlfriend and start planning his wedding? I expect he found that photo of Sunrise Cottage ages ago, only at the time it didn't suit him to act on it.

I hate to admit it, but despite everything, when Jayden drove away in the Peugeot, a tiny piece of my heart went with him. Will I never learn?

The newspaper finds its way to the recycling box. I find my way upstairs to my studio. Picking up a brush, I run the soft sable bristles across my fingertip to loosen them. But I don't make it to the easel, because now the epiphany comes crashing in, hitting me like a cascade from a powerful waterfall.

18

I throw myself at Max as he opens the door, startling myself as much as him. But this is no time to stop and think. I've done all the thinking I need to do.

'I'm not going back to London,' I mumble into his chest. 'Sunrise Cottage is where I belong.'

'That's the best news I've had, ever,' Max says.

And before either of us knows what's happening, our mouths meet and we're kissing as if our lives depend on it.

Later — don't ask me how much later, I couldn't guess at it — I find out something which casts a cloud over my elation when I hear about Max and Sarah's plans to sell Robin Hill, which of course are for the very best of reasons. We're in the downstairs room Max calls the snug when he tells me this, side by side on a rather uncomfortable leather sofa of indeterminate vintage, which I can't fail to notice has a price ticket attached to one leg.

I stay quiet for a moment, thinking how stupid and arrogant I've been to assume that Max would factor me into his life plans. After all, it wasn't so long ago I was insisting we treat this as a summer fling, nothing more.

'I'm staying and you're leaving, then,' I manage to say. '*C'est la vie*.' I give a little shrug and a smile.

'Oh, Violet.' Max sighs, and raises his eyes. 'Haven't you got it yet? Wherever you are, that's where I want to be, too.'

'*Really?*'

Max laughs. 'Yes, really. I could put the sale off — Sarah would be fine with that — but I'd rather not. There's no reason for her to borrow from her parents to buy the shop for any longer than she has to.'

'Of course you mustn't put it off. It must be such a relief, knowing Sarah's better and getting her life back on track.'

I mean every word of this, even though it looks as if the rails carrying my own life along have suddenly warped. Whatever Max says about wanting to be where I am, the practicalities will kick in, eventually. I'll be at Sunrise Cottage and he will be . . . where? He answers this for me.

'It'll take ages to get it sold, anyway. These things always do. Meanwhile, I'll look for a place to rent — in Fold if possible, or as near as I can get.'

My heart performs a little skip. But I want the best for Max. I don't want him to feel restricted because of me. We have, after all, only known each other for a relatively short time, although it doesn't feel that way.

'You could do your antiques thing anywhere. I know you've got the shop in Little Barton, but you could get rid of that and get another one.'

Max pretends to think hard, putting his head on one side and placing a finger over his mouth. I notice a twinkle in his eye.

'Nope. Has to be here.'

'What about all your stuff? Where will it go?'

'This is the nudge I need to get it sorted. I'll make a huge effort and stick most of it up for auction. The rest . . . what I don't need in my own place, I'll put into store.'

'I could help,' I say, thinking about the size of Robin Hill, the amount of stuff it contains and what a mammoth task Max faces.

'Thanks, but you don't need to. A couple of mates of mine will pitch in if push comes to shove. But I've been thinking of taking on another assistant for the business anyway, someone to come with me to auctions and so on. They could help with clearing the house. I've managed so far by employing casual labour on a one-off basis when I need it, but I need somebody regular.'

'But not the knocker-boy type.' I wink, and Max laughs.

And then he narrows his eyes, and I

sense we're heading into choppier waters.

'Did Jayden leave willingly, in the end?'

I told Max earlier about the saga with the car, but I didn't elaborate. Max, however, looks a bit worried.

'Not exactly. He had no choice, though, once I'd virtually kicked him out. We're done for good, and he knows it. Actually, he did me a favour, turning up on my doorstep. He made me think about London, and what I had there — besides him, I mean — and I realised I won't miss any of it. I love teaching and I need to do that, but there'll be openings in and around Sussex. I can't work at The Rose and Crown for ever, though it'll do for now.'

'I'll miss your smiling face behind the bar.'

'Oh, I'm sure you'll see more than enough of it elsewhere.'

I kiss Max lightly on the mouth. He returns the kiss with one on my forehead.

'I'm not going to have any more contact with Sarah, once Robin Hill is sold,' he says, after a moment.

'I hope that's not on my account. You seem to get on well with her. I wouldn't want you to cut her off because of me.'

'No, it's time. Sarah feels the same, I'm sure. We are divorced for a reason.'

A weight lifts from my shoulders. It was easy to be magnanimous about Max's ex-wife before, but the stakes are higher now.

'What would you like to do?' Max suddenly stands up and goes to the window to peer out. 'Shall we go out?'

I join him at the window and peer out too. 'It's raining.'

'Oh yes, so it is.'

'Let's not, then.'

'Are you hungry?'

'Not especially.'

'Neither am I,' Max says. 'We will be later, though. We can go out then.'

'We can.'

My arms find their way around him. He holds me, and we stand there, gazing out at the bright green lawn and the glowering sky above.

After a while, he turns me gently to face him, resting his hands on my shoulders.

'Do you know something, Miss Violet Brooke?'

'What's that, then?'

'I love you.'

I smile.

I don't say it back. But I have a feeling it won't be long before I do.

19

December
Fold, Sussex

I saw Olivia Morton today. I was in the car park of the big supermarket on the main road, and I'd just loaded my shopping into the boot and was wheeling my trolley back when I happened to look up, and there she was, also pushing an empty trolley and heading in my direction.

She saw me at precisely the same moment, a moment in which time stood still while we both wondered what came next, and then I smiled and she carried on walking towards me.

'Hello, Olivia,' I said.

'Violet, I'm so sorry for what I did. I wanted to come and apologise at the time, but I thought it was best I stayed away. And Max, well, he was so understanding . . . '

She looked so miserable and embarrassed that my heart went out to her.

I reached across my trolley and touched her on the arm. 'Olivia, it's all in the past. Please don't be upset about it any more. I'm not.'

'That's very good of you,' she said, her voice small. 'I always liked you and I genuinely wanted to be friends, but all that silly stuff in my head took over, and, well . . . '

'Oh, don't, please,' I said. 'It doesn't matter any more. Olivia, are you okay, though?'

For a second I wanted to retract that question. She was looking far from okay, and I didn't want to start up anything that would embarrass the two of us even more. But then her expression lightened.

'I'm good, thanks. I'm still a work in progress, but I'm getting there. With help.'

She smiled shyly, and I followed her line of sight across the car park to where a man who looked to be older than Olivia, late-forties maybe, was bouncing a small child in a red anorak on his shoulders — Anna. She kept pulling his beanie hat down over his eyes, and giggling.

'That's Peter,' Olivia said, in that wide-eyed conspiratorial way women talk to one another. 'I found him on the internet.' She laughed. 'Well, what's a girl to do?'

I laughed too. And then for want of something else to say, I asked her where she was living now.

'Not far.' She named a village about five miles from Little Barton, in the opposite direction from Fold.

'That's good, then.'

I asked after Anna, but it was clear that she didn't want to talk for too long, which I understood as I was feeling the same. We parked our trolleys, and as I said goodbye, I was thinking how much things can change in a short space of time.

I'm standing at my front window

now, my thoughts still vaguely on Olivia, when I hear my phone beep a message. I go through to the kitchen and pick it up from the table. Max. *Who else?* 'What shall I get your Mum for Christmas?'

It's Saturday, and Max has gone Christmas shopping. He hasn't said where, but I'm hoping it's somewhere with decent shops.

I text back. 'Use your imagination,' adding a smiley with a wicked, toothy grin.

Back comes a smiley with its tongue poking out. 'Very helpful. What if I haven't got any?'

'Get a book token.'

I sign off with a kiss. Three kisses come back. Honestly, if Max doesn't stop texting, he'll never get anything bought at all. I told him my parents won't expect presents from him, but he's keen to do the right thing, and that's so sweet.

Mum and Dad are coming down for Christmas. I haven't got room to put them up here, but Fred has let them have a room at The Rose and Crown, and I'll be attempting to cook dinner for the four of us. My first Christmas at Sunrise Cottage! I get a little thrill of excitement whenever I think about it.

Lizzie warned me to place my order for the turkey early, as the butcher in the high street is very popular at this time of year. She wasn't kidding. I stopped off there on my way back from the supermarket this morning and found a queue snaking halfway along the street, and that's only for the orders. Goodness knows what it will be like when I have to go and collect the bird. I think I'll send Max.

He doesn't live with me, although for the amount of time he spends here, he might as well. He rents the top half of a converted Victorian house in a leafy private road that runs parallel to the high street. It's perfect for him, as Sunrise Cottage is perfect for me. I like having it all to myself, and Max understands that.

Besides, there's no hurry to change things. Max is going nowhere, he assures me, which is his indirect way of letting me know I can trust him. And I do. Which is just as well because I love him to the stars and back.

My phone doesn't beep any more. Max has got down to business, and I must, too. Next Tuesday is our last art class until after New Year, and I must work out a new schedule for when we start again, so I can hand it out. And then I shall do the same for the Friday morning classes I run in Little Barton, and the evening classes I take at the community college. I don't work at The Rose and Crown any more — I don't have the time, with my teaching commitments and my own painting — but we're regulars there now, Max and I.

That sounds so middle-aged!

Seriously, I do wonder what I've come to, sometimes. Occasionally, I think I might have been wrong to take myself out of London and, as Jayden would put it, bury myself in the countryside. But the feeling doesn't last long.

Speaking of Jayden, he's sent me several invitations to private gallery showings and other places where he exhibits. I haven't accepted any yet. But I might, one day.

I might do a lot of things, one day. For now, I love my life and I love Max. And that's as real as it gets.

We do hope that you have enjoyed reading this large print book.

Did you know that all of our titles are available for purchase?

We publish a wide range of high quality large print books including:
Romances, Mysteries, Classics
General Fiction
Non Fiction and Westerns

Special interest titles available in large print are:
The Little Oxford Dictionary
Music Book, Song Book
Hymn Book, Service Book

Also available from us courtesy of Oxford University Press:
Young Readers' Dictionary
(large print edition)
Young Readers' Thesaurus
(large print edition)

For further information or a free brochure, please contact us at:
Ulverscroft Large Print Books Ltd.,
The Green, Bradgate Road, Anstey,
Leicester, LE7 7FU, England.
Tel: (00 44) **0116 236 4325**
Fax: (00 44) **0116 234 0205**

Other titles in the
Linford Romance Library:

ROMANTIC DOCTOR

Phyllis Mallett

1968: As a doctor at St Jermyn's Hospital, Ann Barling's work is her life, and it seems like romance has passed her by completely. She may as well admit to herself that she's now a confirmed spinster. When she returns to work after a holiday, however, change is afoot in the form of newly hired Dr David Hanbury. He has a reputation, and seems determined to add Ann to his list of conquests. But she's having none of it . . .

CHRISTMAS AT COORAH CREEK

Janet Gover

English nurse Katie Brooks is spending Christmas at Coorah Creek. She was certain that leaving London was the right decision, but her new job in the outback is more challenging than she ever imagined. Scott Collins rescued her on her first day and has been a source of comfort ever since. But he no longer calls the town home — it's too full of bad memories, and he doesn't plan on sticking around long. Scott needs to leave. Katie needs to stay. They have until Christmas to decide their future . . .

DATE WITH DANGER

Bonnie spends carefree summers in the Welsh seaside resort where her mother runs a guesthouse. But things will change after she meets Patrik, a young Hungarian funfair worker. Both she and her friend Kay find love in the heady whirl of the fair — and are also fast learning how people they thought they knew can sometimes conceal secrets. As Patrik moonlights for one of her mother's friends, Bonnie fears that he may be heading into danger . . .